TERRIER TRANSGRESSIONS

PET WHISPERER P I

MOLLY FITZ

Editor: Megan Harris
Cover Designer: Lou Harper, Cover Affairs
Proofreader: Alice Shepherd

WHISKERED MYSTERIES
https://whiskeredmysteries.com/

ABOUT THIS BOOK

I'm finally coming to terms with the fact I can speak to animals, even though the only one who ever talks back is the crabby tabby I've taken to calling Octo-Cat. What I haven't quite worked out is how to hide my secret...

Now one of the associates at my law firm has discovered this strange new talent of mine and insists I use it to help defend his client against a double murder charge. To make things worse, Octo-Cat has no intention of helping either of us.

Our only hope rests on a spastic Yorkie named Yo-Yo, who hasn't quite figured out his owner is dead. Can we find a way to get Yo-Yo to help solve the murder without breaking his poor doggie heart?

* * *

To anyone who wishes she could talk to her animal best friend... Well, what's stopping you?

Hi, I'm Angie Russo, and I have a talking cat for a pet. Well, he only talks to me, but still. A few months have passed since he came to live with me following the murder of his owner—a sweet old lady who was poisoned by a member of her own family in a greedy inheritance grab.

Since then, Octo-Cat and I have been settling into our new life as roommates, and he's nice to me more often than not just so long as I feed him his breakfast on time and never, ever call him "kitty." He's even learned how to use his iPad to call me on FaceTime so we can check in with each other while I'm at work.

Yes, *his* iPad.

Have I mentioned just how spoiled he is?

Not only does he have his own tablet—and a trust fund, too—but he insists on drinking Evian fresh from the bottle and will only eat certain flavors of Fancy Feast when served on specific dishes and according to his rigorously kept, though fully unnecessary, schedule.

I have to admit he's grown on me, something I honestly never thought would happen. I even kind of like my job as a paralegal at Fulton, Thompson and Associates these days. Things have been pretty interesting since the Fultons left town rather abruptly and our firm lost its senior most partner.

A cutthroat competition as to who will take his place has ensued. Until Mr. Thompson decides whom he'd like to promote, though, we're simply Thompson and Associates. Lots of candidates—both from within our firm and from outside—have been passing through our office in hopes of securing the coveted position at Blueberry Bay's most respected law firm, but Thompson is having a hard time making up his mind.

Can't say I blame him. I definitely wouldn't want to be in his shoes.

Our firm is now a bit infamous following the surprising murder involving one of its partners and his family. Everyone wants the scoop, but Mr. Thompson has made it very clear: we aren't supposed to discuss what happened with anyone.

In the meantime, he has hired a new associate to help keep up with the newly increased workload. Charles Longfellow, III, came to us highly recommended with a great resume and even better looks.

It's been a while since I've had a crush but—boy —do I have it bad for Charlie. He's got this thick, wavy hair that falls in a perfect dark swoop on his forehead. He's tall, like *maybe-played-basketball-in-high-school-but-probably-not-in-college* tall, and you could easily get lost in his deep green eyes. I know, because I already have a few times.

Yes, as much as I usually prefer books to boys, I often find myself a bit twitterpated whenever Charles is near. That's probably how I made such a colossal mistake in the first place...

Now I'm being blackmailed about my biggest secret, the fact that I can talk to animals.

The worst part? I kind of like it.

I should probably start at the beginning, huh?

Well, here goes nothing...

* * *

cto-Cat called me via FaceTime just before noon. I was at the office, of course, but since he knew not to call unless it was an emergency, I decided to put my research on hold to answer him. Besides, almost everyone had left the firm for an early lunch meeting, leaving me more or less alone in the building.

"What do you need?" I asked after scanning the premises just in case I wasn't as alone as I'd thought. Normally I took my calls with Octo-Cat in the bathroom, but one of the junior associates had been holed up in there for at least half an hour before he left—and I definitely wanted to avoid whatever disaster scenario he'd left behind.

"There's a fly in my Evian," my cat complained with a keening mewl. His face looked utterly scandalized as he leaned in close to the camera.

"Oh, you poor thing," I cooed while rolling my eyes just out of his view. Octo-Cat was definitely too spoiled for his own good sometimes, but then again, I received a five-thousand-dollar monthly allowance for his care, so I really couldn't complain too much.

"My thoughts exactly," he answered with a grimace and a sigh. "I need you to come home immediately to rectify this situation."

"I can't. I'm at work," I reminded him with a beleaguered sigh of my own while clicking through my overfull email inbox idly.

Octo-Cat growled when he noticed he didn't have my full attention. "I thought you were supposed to only be going part-time now?"

Why was I constantly explaining my life choices to a cat? He rarely remembered what I told him, anyway. We'd had this exact same conversation about my work at least three times already. Rehashing it now felt like the ultimate exercise in futility.

Still, it was easier to explain yet again than to deal with one of his hissy fits.

"Yes, technically I am part-time," I explained patiently. "But I need to help out extra until Thompson finally hires a new partner. It's been really busy around here, and unfortunately I just don't have time to stop home and pour you a new cup of water right now. I'm sorry."

His eyes narrowed, ready to go to war over such a simple thing. "But don't you receive a generous monthly stipend to ensure I'm cared for in the manner to which I am accustomed? Because I most definitely am *not* accustomed to having a wiggly-legged fly swimming in my Evian."

Once again, it was easier to cave than it was to argue for hours or days on end. *"Aargh,* fine. I'll send Nan by to pour you some more water. Happy?"

He yawned, which only annoyed me more. "Not exactly. It will take me days to recover from this horrible event. Could you make sure Nan knows she needs to throw out the contaminated cup?"

"You are a cat," I said between clenched teeth. "You are supposed to be a fearsome hunter, not a spoiled baby. You know, other cats even—"

"Angie?" a deep, dreamy voice broke into the middle of our conversation.

Oh, no, no, no. Everyone was supposed to be gone!

I spun around in my chair to find none other than Charles Longfellow, III standing behind me and gawking over my shoulder at the image of Octo-Cat on my phone screen.

"Um, hi, Charles." I tittered nervously as I pushed the button to end our call, but it was too late. He'd already heard and seen more than enough to figure out my secret. The best I could hope for now is that he would think one or both of us had gone crazy.

I took it as a good sign that he stood looking at me as if I'd sprouted a second head. Perhaps that would have been less strange than what he'd really walked in on.

"Is everything all right?" he asked, raising one thick eyebrow in my direction. The air suddenly felt impossibly thin like the office had been transported to the top of the nearest mountain.

I nodded, desperate for Charles to go away and stop questioning me. "Perfectly all right. Thanks," I lied, wishing I'd inherited Nan's legendary acting skills. As it was, I could tell my colleague wasn't fooled by my feeble attempts to downplay the situation.

Sure enough, his voice dripped with sarcasm as he said, "Really? Because it seemed like your cat needed some help with his..." A delicious smile crept across his face, stretching from one high cheek bone to the next. "Evian? Is that right?"

My mouth fell open from shock, but no additional words came out to explain away the freak show my crush had just witnessed.

"Well?" he prompted, widening his eyes at me.

"Were you or were you not just having a conversation with your cat?"

I tucked my hair behind my ears and swallowed hard before stumbling over my answer. "Um, I call him sometimes when I'm away. He has separation anxiety so..." I gave him my most ingratiating smile, but it didn't seem to work. I was seriously outmatched here.

"But it sounded like maybe he was talking back to you," Charles insisted. "Like you were having an actual conversation with each other."

I blinked hard as I stammered, "What? No, don't be silly. Of course I can't talk to animals. I mean, who can?"

"You, apparently," Charles said, narrowing his gaze at me. Clearly he wasn't going to let me off the hook until I revealed the one thing I most wanted to hide.

I swallowed the giant lump that had become lodged in my throat, then broke out in hysterical laughter. *"Gotcha!* I can't believe you fell for my little office prank."

Charles shoved both hands in his pockets and rocked back and forth on his heels, but didn't say anything.

Oh my gosh. Why wasn't he saying anything?

My heart galloped like a wild stallion as my nervous laughter fell away.

Charles studied me for a long time, and stupidly I couldn't bring myself to look away. "You're coming with me," he said.

"What?" I crossed my arms over my chest in defiance. "No. I have too much work to catch up on here."

He placed his palms on my desk and leaned down so our faces were only a few inches apart. Given pretty much any other circumstance, I'd have enjoyed having his gorgeous face so near to mine.

As it was now, though? I was absolutely terrified.

"You're coming with me," he repeated with a devilish grin. "Unless you want me to tell everyone what I saw."

I gulped. "Everyone?"

"Everyone," he confirmed before returning to his full height and straightening his tie.

Completely bewildered and unable to see any practical alternative, I rose to join Charles.

"Excellent," he said, leading me to the door and motioning for me to go through it.

I turned back to study him. "Where are we going?"

"My place," he answered coolly as we strode through the parking lot toward his car. Charles had never invited me anywhere before, especially not his apartment. Unfortunately, something told me I wouldn't like what was waiting for me there one bit.

2

About five minutes after leaving the office, Charles and I pulled up to the Cliffside apartment complex. I was surprised to find that he lived in the budget apartments rather than the nicer condos on the other side of town. Normally, Cliffside was for newly graduated students or those who were otherwise just passing through.

As an attorney, Charles could easily afford somewhere nicer—and safer, too. Crime rarely occurred in Glendale, but when it did, nine times out of ten it happened here. As a criminal defense attorney, perhaps he wanted to be closer to his client base. Still, most of the crimes our firm dealt with fell under the category of white-collar crime.

With its stained carpeting and peeling paint, Cliffside was anything but white collar.

Did Charles living here mean he wasn't planning on making Blueberry Bay his long-term home? Was he just passing through like so many of the others who lived in this run-down cluster of buildings?

Even though he was kind of blackmailing me, I hoped he'd stick around a bit more permanently. Despite everything, I still liked him and preferred his company to the others at the firm. Lately, Bethany and I had formed a tentative friendship, but we often found it hard to relate to one another. We just came from two very different worlds.

Despite his fancy name, perhaps Charles and I weren't so different, after all. No, I hadn't grown up poor, but Nan had raised me to be humble even as others were showering me with praise. Her mantra had always been that the stage was for stars, and real life was for real people.

Maybe Charles had grown up under similar guidance, although Cliffside was a little more "real life" than even I preferred.

He'd remained tight-lipped on the drive over and stayed quiet still as he led me up the stairs to the third floor.

"This is me," he said, turning his key in the door.

I shrugged and followed him in.

Immediately we were greeted by a hyper, barking dog, who was so excited to see us he piddled right on the floor at our feet.

"Sorry about that!" Charles cried, grabbing a roll of paper towels from the nearby counter. "He just gets a little excited sometimes."

"I'll say." I politely patted the little dog on the head but resisted the urge to pick him up, seeing I was in no mood to be peed on today.

Something struck me as odd, though. Charles had already been in town for at least a month, but a quick glance around his apartment showed more unopened boxes than actual furniture or home decor. So, how did he already have a dog? And what did it do all day while he put in the long hours Thompson required of all his associates?

Charles finished cleaning up the mess, washed his hands, and motioned for me to make myself comfortable on the lone futon that sat against the living room wall.

"Where's all your stuff?" I asked conversationally, feeling more than a little unnerved when he sat down beside me on the much too short futon.

The terrier also hopped up when he patted the seat beside him.

He just shrugged, not seeming the least bit embarrassed by my question. "I sold everything before moving east and haven't had the time to pick up much since arriving."

That made sense. He'd come to Maine by way of California, and as far as I knew, he didn't have any family nearby. Why anyone would want to leave guaranteed sunny weather to hole up in small-town Maine, I'd never understand, but still, I was happy to have him here in Blueberry Bay.

The little dog spun in happy circles, racing from Charles's lap to mine and back again and again. The poor thing was obviously deprived of the regular attention he needed.

"If you're so busy, then why do you have a dog? That isn't really fair to him." I didn't mean to sound accusing, but I knew very well from Octo-Cat that animals hated being left alone all day while their owners pursued lives outside the home. No wonder the little guy peed on the floor the moment he came through the door.

"No, I've only had him for a little while," he said with a frown. "And before you can say anything more, I know I don't have time for a dog but... well, it's kind of a long story, and it's why I asked you here."

My curiosity was definitely piqued now, but first, I had to clarify one thing. "You didn't ask me here," I said with a knowing look. "You forced me."

His handsome face pulled down in a frown. "I'm sorry. Really, I am. It's just.. I didn't know how else to get you to come, and I'm kind of desperate here." At least he had the decency to appear apologetic now.

I nodded even though I didn't really understand what he was talking about yet. Obviously, *he* didn't understand that I would have been more than willing to follow him anywhere if only he'd asked nicely.

Charles stroked the tan and gray, silky-coated dog and launched into his story. "This is Yo-Yo. He's not mine. I found him, actually."

I immediately went into fix-it mode. "How long ago? Did you call the shelter? I'm sure someone's really missing him and hoping he'll come home."

Charles shook his head and cleared his throat, glancing from me to Yo-Yo before he said, "No. His owners are dead."

I scooted a little farther from him on the futon.

"What? How could you possibly know that if he's just some dog you found?"

"The address listed here." He thumbed the tag on the Yorkie's collar. "And I know his owners are dead because I'm defending the person accused of their murder."

Well, I'd heard more than enough now. Jumping to my feet, I cried, "Whoa, whoa, whoa. I may not be the one who's taken an oath of ethics, but this seems really, really wrong. What are you hoping to accomplish by keeping this poor dog hostage?"

Charles stood, too, holding Yo-Yo against his chest with one arm and reaching the other toward me. I yanked myself away before he could make contact, though. The last thing I needed was my batty hormones intervening here.

"My client didn't kill Yo-Yo's owners," he said, his eyes begging me to understand. "He's innocent."

"Yeah, everyone says they're not guilty, but you know what? Usually, they are." I briefly considered grabbing Yo-Yo and making a run for it. That poor, little dog. First his owners had been murdered, then he'd somehow inexplicably wound up with the man defending their killer.

"No, it's not like that," Charles insisted. "*I know* he didn't do it, but the evidence against him, it's bad. Like I said, I'm desperate here. So when I saw you talking to your cat, I thought maybe, just maybe, you could be the answer to my prayers. You could save an innocent man from jail and help get justice for Yo-Yo's owners, too."

I considered denying my ability, insisting that there was no way I could do what he was asking for, but Charles just looked so needy—and Yo-Yo also chose that exact moment to whimper and stare at me with sparkling, little doggie eyes...

"*Ugh,* fine!" I shouted, sinking back down onto the futon. "I'll see what I can do."

Relief washed over Charles's face as he lowered himself beside me. "Thank you. You're a lifesaver!"

"Yeah, well, I haven't actually done anything yet," I grumbled. There was absolutely nothing about this situation I liked.

"The fact that you're willing to try means everything," Charles said, and for the briefest of moments something passed between us.

Love?

Longing?

That special bond between a blackmailer and his blackmailee?

Really, I had no idea.

He stood again, then set Yo-Yo on the futon

beside me. The dog jumped on my lap where he immediately began licking my face, his tail wagging wildly with each lap.

"Hey, Yo-Yo," I said, completely unsure of myself. The only animal I'd ever actually carried on a conversation with was Octo-Cat, and he'd talked to me first. This thing right now with Yo-Yo felt crazy, unnatural, and uncomfortable by comparison. Still, I had to try for the sake of Charles and his client. And for Yo-Yo, too.

"I understand you lost your owners," I said slowly with an even voice. "Can you tell me what happened?"

The Yorkie continued licking my face without any signs of slowing down, so I picked him up and put him on the floor to see if it could help him focus.

"What happened to your owners?" I asked again. "Did someone murder them?"

Yo-Yo yipped merrily and hopped back up on the futon beside me. Now he decided it was a good time to douse my hand in a slobber bath.

"What did he say?" Charles asked eagerly. His eagerness made this whole thing that much more frustrating. I'd always hated letting people down. Yes, even when they were blackmailing me, I guess.

"He barked," I said simply.

"Yes, but what did it mean?"

"I don't know," I admitted honestly.

His face fell. "But I thought you could talk to animals?"

"I talk to my cat, but that's it."

"So why can't you talk to Yo-Yo?" This was the hundred-thousand-dollar question. I'd stopped questioning my sanity when it came to my ability to talk to Octo-Cat but still had no idea why I could speak to him or what the extent of my powers might be.

I raised my palms and shrugged. "I don't know, but I'm trying."

"Well, try harder," he urged. "It's really, really important."

"I *am* trying," I muttered to Charles through gritted teeth, then turned back to Yo-Yo with my most pleasant expression. "Hey, there, little guy. If you could talk to me, it would be a huge help. Maybe start by telling me what you really think of this guy you're living with now?"

I hooked a thumb toward Charles and made a goofy face, which resulted in Yo-Yo grabbing hold of my sweater and giving it a firm tug.

"Hey, stop!" I cried, but this only made him tug

harder. When I finally managed to wrestle my shirt away from him, it had been stretched beyond repair. I leaped to my feet so he couldn't destroy any other parts of me before we were through here.

"What did he say?" Charles asked, hope reflecting in his dark eyes.

"He said you've got the wrong girl," I answered. "And that he liked my sweater but still thought it deserved to die a horrible, untimely death."

Charles deadpanned. "Just like his owners, huh?"

Okay, now I felt bad, but it didn't change anything about my inability to speak with Yo-Yo. I'd tried. It hadn't worked. It was time to move on.

"I don't know what he said or even if he said anything," I explained, hoping Charles would finally take me at my word. "I guess I can't talk to dogs."

"But you can talk to cats?"

I shrugged noncommittally, but he seemed to interpret this as my agreement.

"Great," he said, shuffling through the items in a junk drawer before extracting a long, black leash. "C'mon, Yo-Yo. We're going for a walk," he cried in a slightly higher pitched voice that made me forget my irritation for a moment—but only a moment. "Want to go for a walk?"

"And I'm going back to work," I said, traipsing toward the door. "Drop me off on your way to wherever it is the two of you are going."

"Sorry, can't," Charles answered while the Yorkie ran furious, barking circles around the apartment to convey his enthusiasm. "We need you to come with us."

I crossed my arms and eyed them both suspiciously. "Why?"

"Because we're going to your house to talk to your cat," Charles explained, grabbing Yo-Yo into his arms and clipping on the leash.

To my house?

Crud. Octo-Cat was definitely not going to like this.

3

Less than two miles stretched between Charles's apartment complex and my rental home, which meant we were in one place almost as soon as we'd left the other.

I opened the door to find Octo-Cat waiting for me with a rapturous look upon his face.

"Finally!" he cried. "I've been so thirsty." His expression quickly changed to outrage, though, when Yo-Yo nosed his way into the house and gave Octo-Cat a big, wet kiss right on the nose.

Charles pulled back on the leash, then lifted the visiting dog into his arms.

Octo-Cat shook with fury as a bead of drool dripped down his face and onto the carpet below.

"Why would you do this to me? Haven't I already been through enough today? First the fly and now a-a-a *dog?*" he spat out that last word as if it were the foulest curse word he could imagine.

"What's he saying?" Charles asked with rapt interest.

"He's mad at me," I admitted. "And he's not happy about Yo-Yo being here, either."

Octo-Cat arched his back and hissed. "You can say that again," he muttered before jumping onto the kitchen table.

"Just give me a minute here," I whispered to Charles before joining my irate tabby in the kitchen.

Octo-Cat took a giant leap from the table to the counter, then sat with his tail flicking back and forth wildly. "Unbelievable," he growled without so much as looking at me.

I knew I was in the wrong here, but I also had no other choice but to comply with Charles's wishes. If anyone else found out about my special ability to talk to cats, I'd lose my job, be made a laughing stock, and possibly have to move away from the only home I've ever known to start life over with a clean reputation.

Hopefully Octo-Cat would understand that my hands were tied once I had the chance to explain a bit more. First, though, I needed to find a way to give Charles what he wanted. Once I did, the threat hanging over my head would be eradicated, and Octo-Cat could go back to being mad at me for the usual reasons.

I grabbed a fresh bottle of Evian and a clean china tea cup from the cupboard. The cup came from the set we'd inherited from his late owner Ethel and was used for the sole purpose of offering Octo-Cat his daily libations. After presenting the fresh water to him, I made quick work disposing of the dead fly.

He took one quick lap from the dish, then trotted off to my bedroom without so much as a thank you.

"You're welcome!" I called after him with a scowl. Jeez, it felt like no one appreciated me today.

"So what now?" Charles asked, bending down to unleash Yo-Yo.

"No, wait," I cried, but unfortunately it was too late.

The Yorkie immediately darted into my bedroom, barking manically the whole way. A dreadful hiss-growl-meow hybrid reverberated through the house, and a second later Octo-Cat appeared with his tail poofed out so large that it resembled that of a raccoon.

"I hate you!" he screamed, tearing through the house as the dog gave chase.

"Grab him!" I yelled to Charles, who made a leap for the rambunctious animal and missed.

"Hey, Yo-Yo!" I called, racing back toward the kitchen. "Want a treat?"

The Yorkie immediately turned in his tracks and trotted after me, releasing a joyous series of high-pitched barks. I reached into the fridge and grabbed a slice of lunch meat to offer him as a treat just as Charles managed to re-clip the leash to his collar.

"Well, that was an experience," he said with a weary chuckle.

"I wouldn't laugh if I were you," I told him. "It's going to take forever for my cat to forgive me now."

Charles stared at me in confusion.

"If he won't forgive me, then he also won't help. Don't you know anything about cats?" I grumbled, despite the fact that I hadn't really known anything about them myself until a few months prior.

He looked properly chastised as he hung his head and let out a giant sigh. "Sorry. What should we do?"

"We aren't going to do anything just yet. *You* are going to take Yo-Yo outside, and I guess I'll go offer up my firstborn in a last-ditch attempt to get Octo-Cat to talk to me."

Charles began to smile but quickly retracted it immediately upon seeing the stone-cold serious expression on my face.

"Uh, okay. C'mon, Yo-Yo," he said, yanking the little dog toward the door.

"Don't come in until I tell you it's okay," I shouted after them.

"It's never going to be okay," Octo-Cat hissed, emerging from wherever it was he'd been hiding. "Why would you do that to me?"

"I'm sorry. I didn't want to," I rushed to explain. "He made me."

Octo-Cat wagged his tail, which had mostly returned to its normal size. "So you sold me out for a pretty face," he cried. "I thought we were friends! I thought we were family!"

My heart clenched. Normally I didn't let his dramatics get to me, but this particular reprimand cut deep. This is what I got for confiding my work-place crush to my cat. He was thankfully getting better at telling humans apart and could accurately guess gender about four times out of five now. Of course, when I needed him to identify a murderer, he was hopeless, but when it came to figuring out my crush? Sure, *that* was no problem.

"I didn't want to," I repeated yet again. "He walked in on us FaceTiming earlier and forced me to help him."

Octo-Cat scoffed. "So he walked in on you. *Lie!* Seriously, Angela, how hard is that?"

He rarely used my name, and even more rarely my birth name. Oh, yeah, I was in serious trouble now. Someone would most definitely be waking up to vomit in her shoes tomorrow—and, sadly, that somebody was me.

"Look," I said, trying to reason with him. "Regardless of whether you would have handled things differently, we're here now. Charles wants us to talk to that dog to learn about how his owners died so that he can better defend his client who is being wrongfully accused of their murder."

Octo-Cat nodded but maintained his cold, narrow gaze. He'd been watching a lot of *Law & Order* reruns lately in an effort to better understand my job, and I was glad to see he'd learned enough to keep up with the legalese required to understand the situation.

"Okay, fine," he said after a thoughtful pause. "But why didn't you just talk to the dog yourself? Why did you need to drag me into this circus?"

"Because," I whined, wishing that he could just take me at my word for once in our lives. "I couldn't understand Yo-Yo, and I don't think he could understand me, either."

"Again, why couldn't you have lied? For goodness' sake, Angie, make something up so we can all move on with our lives."

Well, it was nice to know my cat had no problems with lying to get out of a scrape. My morals were less questionable, however. Also, I'd already tried lying to Charles and it hadn't worked.

At this point I had seriously begun to worry about the ramifications of my midday work break. How much time had passed? Had Thompson and the other associates returned to the office and realized I was missing yet?

"I am not going to lie to him," I said, choosing to take the high road. "Especially not about a case. What if his client really is innocent? What if he has to spend the rest of his life in jail because my lie messed up the case? Yeah, no thank you."

Octo-Cat groaned and rolled his eyes, a new human gesture he'd picked up from me. "So what? You need me to translate because you can't speak dog?"

"Yes, please." I clasped my hands in front of me. I wasn't above begging, and Octo-Cat just so happened to love it when I groveled.

He took on a self-important air, glancing down his nose at me. It made his eyes cross, and I had to fight to suppress a laugh. "You know dogs have a much simpler language than cats. It matches their simple minds. If you understand me, then you should definitely be able to talk to Dum-Dum out there."

"So you'll help?" I asked, praying he could see how desperately I needed him.

"Fine, I'll help" he said with a growl. "But you owe me. *Big time.*"

I raced to the door to let Charles and Yo-Yo in before my cat could change his mind. "Keep him on the leash this time," I instructed as they passed back through the threshold into my home. "Better yet, keep him on your lap."

Charles took a seat on my living room couch

with the dog perched on his lap. "What now?" he asked as I took up residence in my arm chair.

"First, promise me that you won't tell anyone about any of this."

He bobbed his head in rapid, enthusiastic agreement. "Yes, I promise."

I nodded, too. "Good. Now remember I don't even know if this is going to work, but give me a few minutes and we'll be able to find out."

Charles fell silent, his eyes fixed squarely on me. It seemed that maybe Octo-Cat frightened him a bit, and that was just fine by me.

I turned to my tabby companion and said, "Would you please ask Yo-Yo what happened to his owners?"

Octo-Cat hopped up onto the coffee table and faced the dog on Charles's lap before repeating the question.

Yo-Yo gave a happy, little yap and began to pant, which my cat translated as, "He says his owners are the nicest people in the whole world and that the guy he is staying with right now is nice, but he misses his family and wants to go home."

"He said all that?" It took Octo-Cat at least ten times longer to translate that than it took Yo-Yo to speak it.

"I told you," Octo-Cat said, taking a quick break to lick at his paw. "Dog language is incredibly simple. What he actually said translates to 'best, miss,' but when dealing with dogs you have to add a ridiculous degree of enthusiasm to get a proper sense of what they want to tell you. It's exhausting, really."

"What are they saying?" Charles asked.

"Shhh," Octo-Cat and I both hissed.

Charles slumped back on the couch and watched us with a mix of intrigue and fear.

Turning back to my cat, I requested, "Would you please ask him if he was present when his owners were murdered?"

When Octo-Cat relayed my question, Yo-Yo let out a long, shrill series of screams and clawed at Charles's lap in a panicked attempt to get away.

"Oh my gosh, what happened?" I cried at the same time Charles asked, "What the heck was that about?"

I looked to Octo-Cat for an explanation.

The cat's eyes widened as he revealed, "He says his owners aren't dead, and that pretending they are is a mean and terrible joke to make."

So much for using Yo-Yo to plan a defense for Charles's client. It sounded as if the little dog were being murdered himself simply by being asked about their deaths. How could we get any useful information from him if he didn't even realize they had died?

One thing was for certain: I wasn't going to be the one to break this poor, sweet doggie's heart.

4

I watched helplessly as Charles raked both hands through his hair in distress.

"I just don't know what to do anymore," he admitted with a deep, guttural groan. "I thought for sure when I saw what you could do that it was fate, that you were meant to help me defend this case."

I leaned forward in my chair and placed a consoling hand on his knee. It was the only part of him I could reach, but still, the minor contact sent a little thrill racing from my fingertips straight to my chest. "Maybe I can find another way to help. There's still one thing that really doesn't make much sense to me, though."

He raised his head to look at me. A series of

wrinkles lined his brow as he waited for what I had to say.

I cleared my throat before asking, "If you're so sure your client didn't do it, then how come you don't have a defense for him outside of talking to the victims' dog?"

He slumped back on his chair and ran a hand through his hair again, releasing the scents of soap and pine into the air. "Because everyone's already decided he's guilty."

"Except you," I said flatly.

Charles sighed. "Seems that way."

"Okay, so walk me through this, then. Can you tell me more about what happened and why everyone's so convinced your client is guilty? Also, I'd love to know how you ended up with this dog."

Octo-Cat settled in on the chair beside me. "Actually, I'd love to know that, too."

We both waited while Charles composed himself enough to tell us the story.

"If he starts this thing with 'it was a dark and stormy night,' I'm going to puke," Octo-Cat remarked with an exaggerated yawn.

"Hush up, you," I said to the impatient tabby at my side before offering Charles an apologetic glance. "Sorry. Go on."

He cocked his head and studied the pair of us for a moment. "What did he say?"

"You don't want to know," I muttered, stroking Octo-Cat with more force than he generally liked as my way of sending him a silent warning.

Charles let his gaze linger on Octo-Cat as he launched into his description of the murder. "It happened in the morning. The victims—their names were Bill and Ruth Hayes—had just put their house on the market. Apparently they'd already had an offer accepted on a new place and needed their old place to move fast, so a big open house was planned for that day. I guess property in their subdivision rarely goes up for sale, so there was a lot of interest. At least a dozen couples arrived to check the place out, and one of them discovered the victims' bodies shoved into the master bedroom closet upstairs."

I took this all in before asking, "Okay, so lots of people means lots of potential suspects. Why did the blame get pegged on your client?"

"The crime scene guys said they'd been dead for close to ten hours before they were discovered the next morning, and it was my client's hammer that was used as the murder weapon. Besides his sister, he was one of the only people who had access to their home and knew the code to disarm the security system." Charles's face was grim as he recounted the details. The more he told me, the more familiar the events started to feel. I hadn't been brought in to research this case for the firm, but I had heard all these details before from another source...

"Wait, is this the Brock Calhoun case? I've seen that all over the news." I wasn't sure whether Charles knew that my mom was the anchor for our local station or that she was part of the reason everyone assumed his client's guilt. I decided not to mention that part. Otherwise, he'd never let me help him, and clearly he needed as much help as he could get right now.

Charles nodded. "He and his sister Breanne were the ones responsible for selling the place. Someone used Brock's hammer to bludgeon the two homeowners to death."

"Ouch. Yeah. It doesn't look good for your client." I sucked air in through my teeth and glanced toward Yo-Yo, who was now snoozing on the floor by Charles's feet. Thank goodness he couldn't understand what we were saying now. No one wants to picture their loved ones meeting such a violent end, and this particular Yorkie seemed less equipped than most to deal with such a harrowing mental picture.

Charles also looked down at Yo-Yo before meeting my eyes again. "Like I said, everyone's already decided he's guilty, and now the community's pressing for a quick conviction and harsh sentencing."

I tried to keep my expression neutral as I asked, "What makes you believe he's innocent?"

"Part of it is the fact that the evidence is largely circumstantial. Another reason is that people seem to have decided he was guilty based on the fact that he wasn't the nicest person during his high school years, and also..." He seemed to debate whether he actually wanted to tell me this next part.

"You can tell me," I said with what I hoped amounted to a reassuring smile.

He shrugged. "Well, it's just a feeling I get when I talk to him. I know he's telling me the truth when he says he didn't do it."

I nudged his knee again and made a funny face. "Is intuition one-oh-one something they're teaching in law school these days?"

My joke didn't even get him to crack a smile.

Octo-Cat, however, sighed and said, "Was that

supposed to be funny? We really need to get you a joke book or something."

Charles hung his head and continued to frown. "I know I'm new to town, but it just seems ridiculous that stupid teenage behavior from nearly ten years ago could cost this guy everything. So what if he bullied some classmates? I mean, it's not great, but it's also not murder."

I nodded. Brock had been a year ahead of me in school and—yeah—he'd been a jerk, but just like Charles, I also had a hard time picturing him as a killer.

"You said the Hayeses were bludgeoned to death with a hammer, right? That seems an awful lot like a crime of passion to me. What possible reason could Brock have had to kill them, especially so brutally and at close range?"

Charles perked up at this. "That's the crux of my defense so far—that he had zero motive even if he had the means and opportunity."

"And the police aren't helping?" I thought back to my encounter with Officer Bouchard and his partner a few months ago. They'd saved my life without even a moment's hesitation. Could the same force really be turning their back on Brock in his hour of need?

Charles laughed bitterly. "If only. Once they made their arrest, they just kind of clocked out. That's really the worst part of all of this. How can the justice system do its job properly if the police don't do theirs?"

"Yeah, yeah, yeah," Octo-Cat complained with an emphatic flick of his tail. "He's still leaving out the most important part. How did he wind up with that doggie menace in the first place?"

"Where does Yo-Yo fit into all of this?" I translated for Charles as I placed a stilling hand on the tabby beside me.

"That's the weirdest part. He was missing on the morning of the open house. Everyone assumed he'd just run away, but when I was driving through the Hayes's neighborhood last week, desperate for any clue or lead I could uncover, I found him waiting on the porch asking to be let in."

Okay, that was weird, but it still didn't explain why Charles had kept him all this time. "And you decided the best thing to do would be to steal him?"

He rushed to defend himself, but I wasn't buying it. "No, no, of course not."

"Then why do you still have him?"

"It was already pretty late that night, so I was going to take him to Animal Control the next morning. Only Thompson called me in early to go over the case, and I really needed his input. So then I decided I would take Yo-Yo in after work."

I couldn't argue with this. After all, Thompson was my boss, too, and I knew how demanding he could be. "Let me guess, it was too late again?"

Charles nodded emphatically. "Exactly, and the longer I hung on to him, the more the little guy began to grow on me. Also, the harder it became to just dump him off at Animal Control, or to confess that I was the one who had him all this time."

"Well, not all this time," I pointed out. Charles had hung on to Yo-Yo for less than a week, so where was he all that time before? How did he just disappear and then show up again as if no time had passed at all?

"A terrible reason to keep a dog," Octo-Cat said with a sneer. "I guess your hots for this guy have to be extinguished now. You can't end up with a dog person, Angela. That just won't do."

Heat pooled in my cheeks from morbid embarrassment, but then I remembered that Charles couldn't understand Octo-Cat—and seriously, thank goodness for that!

"Everything okay?" Charles asked, glancing from me to my cat and back again.

This was the exact moment Yo-Yo chose to wake up from his nap. Upon spotting the cat sitting just a few feet away, he resumed his hyper chain of barks almost as if he'd never stopped in the first place.

"Well, isn't this pleasant?" Octo-Cat growled as he hopped to the top of my chair and took cover, using me as a human shield. "I don't like this dog, and I don't like your boyfriend."

"He's not my boyfriend," I corrected without thinking.

Now Charles was the one blushing. Oh, great.

"Will you please just stop embarrassing me in front of Charles?" I whisper-yelled at the cat.

Octo-Cat laughed but refused to back down or even apologize.

"Anyway," Charles said as he scooped up the noisy terrier. "Do you think you could help with —?" He continued talking, but it was impossible to hear him over Octo-Cat, who decided now was the perfect time to start in on one of his annoying diatribes.

"Charles is far too classy a name for this oaf," he mused. "It sounds more like the name of a cat person, and a cat person would never have tormented me with Dum-Dum the way this guy did."

"Keep your commentary to yourself, please," I begged, trying to focus my attention back on Charles.

"I'm going to give him a new name, one that fits him better."

"Great, tell me about it later," I mumbled to the cat. "Charles, I'm sorry. Would you mind starting over?"

"Sure, I was hoping you could help me with—"

"What might some good nicknames for Charles be? Charlie, Chuck... *Huh.* More like Upchuck, because being around him and his dog make me want to barf up my breakfast."

I had almost managed to drown out Octo-Cat's voice when he shouted at the top of his lungs. "Yes, Upchuck! It's the perfect name for him. Upchuck, Upchuck, Upchuck," he sang in absolute merriment and at the fullest possible volume his tiny kitty lungs could produce.

And he didn't stop after saying it a few times. He'd already repeated this cruel new moniker at least fifty times when Charles asked, "What do all these meows mean? I've never heard a cat talk so much in all my life."

"*Um,* he's just wondering if you have a nickname we could call you by," I hedged. What? My explanation was mostly true. While I wasn't big on bending the truth, I was even less a fan of hurting others' feelings when it was in no way warranted.

Charles broke into a smile at last. "Sure," he said, his eyes lingering on mine. "My grandfather was Charles. My dad was Charlie... And since I'm the third, they call me Chuck. You can, too, when we're not in the office. I mean, if you like that better."

Of course his nickname would be Chuck. Of course it would.

Octo-Cat just about died laughing.

5

Even with our multiple pit stops, Charles—I'm sorry, I just can't bring myself to call him "Chuck"—and I still made it back to the office before the others returned from their long working lunch.

Charles locked himself into his office for the rest of the day, while I did some research on prior cases that could help defend Brock Calhoun from the double murder charge hanging over his head. Charles had probably already pulled every possible case, seeing as he was so desperate he'd now turned to my newly discovered pet whispering abilities to help suss out leads. Still, it felt good to know I was doing something to assist on the case.

Toward the end of the day, the mailman came

and handed me a thick stack of bills, flyers, and correspondence for the office. After discarding the ads and circulars into the recycle bin, I made a round to deliver the letters by hand.

Charles groaned when I brought his to the office he shared with Derek. Previously, another associate named Brad had sat at his desk, but he was fired a few months back for workplace misconduct—which was a gentle way of saying the guy was the biggest, most sexist jerk you could possibly imagine.

"More hate mail, I take it," Charles said as he studied the postmark and sighed. "Great. It's coming all the way from Misty Harbor now."

"Hate mail? You have got to be kidding." I sat down on Derek's empty desk. He must have gone home early after the big lunch meeting. Whatever the case, I was thankful to have some alone time with Charles now. Yes, I'd already forgiven him for the blackmailing that had taken place that morning. Maybe I needed to re-evaluate my life choices, or maybe it was just impossible to stay mad at a guy who already seemed so defeated.

"I wish," he said as he tore his thumb through the top of the envelope and extracted the folded paper inside. His eyes roamed down the page quickly, and then he handed the letter to me. "This is pretty much the usual these days."

The short letter was typed in a large serif font and wasn't signed by its sender. *You should be ashamed of yourself* was the general gist, but it also included threats of picketing the trial and appealing to the bar to get Charles's ability to practice law revoked.

"Is this for real?" I asked, shaking my head as I handed the letter back to him. "People are ridiculous."

"If they're sending me this much mail, I can only imagine how much Brock must be getting." Charles balled up the note and tossed it in the trash.

No wonder he was so desperate to defend his client. I hadn't seen the people in my hometown—and even the neighboring towns, too!—this worked up since a popular football player got suspended for dealing drugs to underclassmen. He lost his college offers, scholarships, and even had his Homecoming King title retroactively pulled.

And back then it was just drugs.

Now we were facing murder, and things definitely didn't look good for Brock. Small towns never forget, which meant that even if he was found innocent, his reputation would be forever tainted and he'd probably have to move somewhere new to start over.

Poor guy.

"It gets even worse," Charles said, his mouth arranged in a firm line. "I just found out the local news station is devoting their entire broadcast tonight to a special they're calling *Brock Calhoun: A Murderer Amongst Us.*"

Ugh, leave it to my mom to go full-on sensational over this.

"I might be able to help with that," I said with a cringe and an apologetic smile.

He turned to me with excitement shining in his eyes. "Of course! Why hadn't I put two and two together before? The sports guy, Roman Russo, you're related, aren't you?"

"Yes," I admitted through clenched teeth. "He's my dad. Also Laura Lee is my mom."

His expression soured instantly. Generally my mom was well-liked all across Glendale and the greater Blueberry Bay region. Usually, though, people didn't find themselves on the receiving end of her passion for investigative journalism.

Most people also didn't realize that our locally famous news anchor was actually my mom, seeing as she decided to keep her maiden name just in case Nan's lingering showbiz connections could help her own career get a leg up.

That strategy had worked well, and Mom had boasted a very successful career pretty much ever since I was in diapers. Lately, though, she seemed to be growing tired of all the puff pieces and human-interest stories that dominated Glendale's news. I hadn't talked to her in a couple weeks, but I could almost guarantee that she saw the Brock Calhoun case as a way of getting national attention —and possibly a better job offer for both her and my dad.

"Let me talk to her," I said with a sigh. "Maybe I can get her to ease up a little."

"More like ease up a lot," Charles said with a groan.

I nodded. "Yes, okay. I'm not sure I can catch her before tonight's story runs, but I promise you I'll do my best."

"Thanks." Charles frowned and shuffled some papers around on his desk, which I took as my dismissal.

Halfway to the door, though, he stopped me. "Angie?"

"Hmmm?" I whipped around, pleasantly surprised by the smile he offered me.

"Thank you," he said in earnest. "I know I kind of pulled you into this case against your will, but it means a lot that you're willing to help me."

"No problem," I said with a giant grin of my own. Yes, I'd definitely forgiven him for the whole blackmail thing now.

Charles returned to the papers on his desk, and I left his office to return to my own work spot near the firm's front door. As soon as I reached my desk, I shot a quick text to my mom:

SOS. We need to talk ASAP. XOXO.

I usually preferred to text in complete sentences and with proper punctuation, but it was a well-known fact that the more acronyms I used, the more likely my mom would be to respond quickly. Sure enough, I received a message back almost as soon as I'd hit *send* on mine.

What's wrong? She included an exploding head emoji and also one that looked like an alien, which I didn't quite understand, given the context. It kind of rankled that my middle-aged mother was more up on the current lingo than I'd ever be.

I drew in a deep breath before composing my next text. I had her attention now, but getting her to agree wouldn't be easy. *Need you to cancel the Brock Calhoun special you're planning for tonight.*

My phone buzzed with an incoming call not even a full minute later.

Mom's voice sounded panicked, which made me feel a bit defensive. "Why do you need me to cancel my report? It's one of the best pieces I've ever put together."

I pinched the bridge of my nose while speaking, hoping it would help to stave off the migraine pressure I felt building in my head. "I'm sure it is, Mom, but he hasn't been put on trial yet. It isn't fair to turn the whole area against him before he even gets a chance to defend himself."

Please understand. Please understand. Please understand.

It was hard to predict how my mom would react. Growing up, we hadn't shared the close relationship that many mothers and daughters do. She worked hard and never deprived me of anything, but it was Nan who had put in the emotional work raising me. Nan had always been the one I came to with my secrets, my dreams, my fears. Mom supported me in everything I did, but she was also so busy living her big life that being a mother sometimes felt too small by comparison.

I think this was a big part of the reason I hadn't settled down myself yet—not just the whole starting a family thing, but also really committing to a single career path. I liked having my options wide open and only being accountable to myself— well, and my cat, too. I couldn't imagine the pressure my mom felt whenever her home and work lives collided, and especially when they crashed into one another as was the case with my request today.

"We all know he did it," my mom said in little more than a whisper. "Besides, I heard my piece might get picked up all across the state and maybe even farther out on the Eastern seaboard, too."

I inhaled sharply before revealing, "Mom, my firm is defending him, and now I'm helping with the case, too."

It took a moment for her to respond. When she did, she didn't seem at all sure of the words she spoke. "Perhaps you could recuse yourself. We all know paralegaling isn't your real passion, but sharing important stories with the public is mine. Please, Angie. I don't want to hurt you, but can't you see that this is my big shot at finally breaking out of local news?"

"I know, and I wouldn't ask unless it was really important."

"We've already been advertising it, too," she said, her voice getting weaker with each syllable.

"So I heard." I racked my brain for a solution that would satisfy both of us, finally landing on something that I thought might work. "Tell you what. Do you think you can hold the story until Friday? That will give us some time to work on the case without the added cloud of bias."

Mom's words came out a little surer. "Okay, but what happens Friday?"

I presented the first option with as much as enthusiasm as I could muster. After all, it would be the better option for both of us, and I thought maybe that saying it aloud would give it more of a chance of actually coming true. "Either we prove beyond a shadow of a doubt that Brock Calhoun is not guilty, and we give you the exclusive right to break our story."

"Or?" Something rustled on the other end of the line, and I pictured my mom twisting nervously in her seat as she waited for me to make my full offer.

"You run it as-is and I won't try to stop you."

The line went silent for a frighteningly long time.

At last, my mother returned, her voice sweet

and placating. "Honey, are you sure? You seem really upset about all of this."

I gulped down my anxiety. The clock had been set, and already it was ticking. "I'm sure. Thank you, Mom. If anyone at the station gets mad at you, send them over to me."

She laughed, and I felt all the stress we'd each been holding bubble up and float away into the sky. "I just might have to do that," she said with a sigh. "I love you, Angie. Good luck on the case," she added before ending the call.

Yes, luck—Charles and I would definitely need it. We'd also need a certain pair of talking animals to get over their hang-ups to help us figure out some new leads. Otherwise, we might as well sign Brock's sentence now, because we seemed to be out of any other reasonable avenues for his defense.

Perhaps I'd stop by the grocery store and pick up some fresh shrimp as a way to bribe Octo-Cat into spending more time with Yo-Yo. Here's hoping my feline friend loved shrimp more than he hated dogs.

awoke the next morning with a growing sense of dread lodged right between my lungs. The weight of knowing that Brock's freedom seemed to now rest squarely on my shoulders made it difficult to catch my breath.

I couldn't let him—or Charles—down. I also wanted to find the real culprit and secure justice for poor Yo-Yo, who still had no idea his owners were even dead.

Despite my vow to never come to the office before nine in the morning, I sucked it up and headed to the firm almost as soon as I could string a coherent thought together.

As expected, only Bethany had arrived before me. I'd never understand why she insisted on showing up so early every single day, but at least she looked happy to see me when I knocked on her office door to say hello.

The cloying and heavy scent of citrus combined with freshly brewed coffee to create a nauseating aroma as I breezed into her office. Bethany may have become a softer, kinder person lately, but the one thing that would never change was her obsession with essential oils. Hey, everyone had their weird little things. I definitely wasn't in any place to judge.

Besides, Bethany was my own personal hero these days.

After I got electrocuted by the old office coffee maker, she brought in a Keurig machine, which she kept in her private space rather than the common area. Honestly, I was still terrified of that horrible appliance in all its forms but—much to my surprise and relief—Bethany had kindly taken to brewing me a cup each morning. I never needed to ask or to work up the courage to press the *brew* button on my own.

Thus her having become one of my favorite people lately.

"Good morning," she said with an alert smile on her fair face. My guess was she'd already imbibed two to three cups before I even arrived. "You're here early."

"Yeah," I said with a tiny wave hello. "Seeing if I can help Charles with the Brock Calhoun case."

Bethany rose to approach the coffee maker, and I was so happy I almost hugged her right then and there. Bethany and I were slowly becoming friends, but making physical contact would probably be more of a detriment than a boon to our relationship. She usually avoided hugs, handshakes, and the like whenever she could. Maybe it was something about being the only female associate at our firm, or maybe it was just her personality. Whatever the case, I knew better than to judge the woman responsible for caffeinating me five days out of seven.

"You know," she said as she popped a morning blend cup into the machine. "I was really surprised Thompson assigned such a prominent case to our newest associate. Honestly, it's one he should have handled himself."

I shrugged. "Maybe everyone else was too busy to add to their workloads right now. We have been getting a lot of business ever since... you know."

She took a couple steps closer to me and lowered her voice. "I know but—and please just keep this between you and me—I had time to help, and I'm pretty sure Derek and some of the others could have made time, too."

"What are you trying to say?"

Bethany dropped her voice even lower. "I'm saying that I think Thompson gave this case to Charles on purpose, knowing he'll probably lose it."

"And?" I may have been awake enough to drag myself to the office, but my real thinking ability wouldn't kick in until after I'd drained my first cup of joe.

"Well, think about it. Charles is brand new to the firm. When he loses what amounts to a more or less impossible case, it'll be easy for Thompson to fire him and move that stigma away from the firm."

"Like a sacrificial lamb?" Even as I questioned her, I knew Bethany was right. Our senior partner definitely wasn't above such underhanded tactics.

Her eyes glowed an unnatural hue as she nodded. "Exactly. That way Thompson gets to keep enjoying our new-found wave of success without having to worry about one notorious trial dragging him down."

That all made perfect sense, but how could Thompson be so sure Charles would lose? He was giving his everything and then some to this case. He could still win it in the end. I raised an eyebrow and asked, "But what if Charles wins?"

"Even better," Bethany answered, grabbing my coffee cup from the machine and placing it directly into my outstretched hands. "Then he'll get to brag about how his firm won the unwinnable, how he discovered Charles almost straight out of law school and recognized his talent instantly. We'll become even more popular, and Thompson will be able to pad his retirement account nicely."

"Well, that's super fun," I muttered before taking an appreciative sip from my mug.

"Isn't it though?" Bethany nodded as she paced across the office to return to her desk. "I think it's nice you're helping Charles. He's going to need every last bit he can get."

Bethany and I chatted about other things for a few minutes, but my mind stayed on what I had just learned about Charles. Did he know his job was on the line, too? Is that why he so badly wanted to win, or did it still come down to his belief in Brock's innocence?

Whatever the case, it wasn't fair for Thompson to move him clear across the country only to set him up to fall on the sword at the first available opportunity. I needed to help him win this case, and not just because the office would feel sad and empty without him...

But also because it was the right thing to do.

* * *

By nine o' clock, the rest of our colleagues had joined us at the office. I snuck into Mr. Thompson's office after giving him a few minutes to settle in.

"Good morning, sir," I said, clasping my hands in front of me and offering my most ingratiating smile. "I have a request if you're not too busy."

Our lone partner glanced up from his computer monitor and looked at me briefly before returning his attention to whatever was displayed on the screen before him. "Go ahead," he said in a way that suggested he would rather not deal with me just then. Still, I had to get his okay before going forward with my plan, whether or not he was in a good mood that day.

"I'd like to devote my week to helping Longfellow with the Calhoun case," I informed him bravely. While our previous partner, Mr. Fulton, had called everyone by their first names, Mr. Thompson only used last names. It was cold and impersonal and part of what made him so scary.

He dropped his hands from the keyboard and raised his eyes to mine, at last giving me his full attention. "Why?"

Luckily, I'd spent the last half hour or so preparing for this conversation and was ready with my response. "Longfellow is doing a great job, but his job is being made more difficult by the media. More specifically, by my mother. Adding me to this case will get her to ease up some while we work out a defense. It could be the difference between a win and a loss for Thompson and Associates on this case."

My boss studied me for a moment before offering a quick nod of agreement. "Good thinking, Russo."

"Thank you, sir," I said, ready to book it out of there and head straight to Charles's office to share the good news.

"Next week you return to business as usual, though," Thompson called after me. And, yes, that was fine, seeing as we really only had until Friday to figure out our defense, anyway.

I ran into Charles just as he was leaving the office he shared with Derek.

"Leaving so soon?" I asked, unable to hide my enthusiasm at officially being assigned to the case.

"Yup. I'm meeting with a client at ten," he informed me as we walked together toward the door.

"If it's Brock Calhoun, then I'm coming, too."

He paused to study me, and those same worried wrinkles from the other day stretched across his forehead.

"Thompson assigned me to the case for the week," I explained with a flippant wave. "Now let's go."

Charles shrugged but didn't argue when I followed him out to his car and climbed into the passenger seat.

"Since I guess you're on the case now," he told me while navigating us toward the state prison where Brock was being held on remand. "I'll share the discovery with you when we get back to the office." He bit his lip and hesitated. It looked as if he'd missed a shave or two, and I hoped my help wasn't too late to keep him from coming undone.

"What?" I asked, eager to know what had him so upset now.

Charles risked a quick glance at me before returning his gaze to the road ahead. "It's pretty gruesome. The crime scene photos, I mean. Are you going to be okay looking at them?"

"I'll be fine," I said, even though I wasn't so sure. I hadn't struggled much with blood and gore before. Heck, I'd even completed a phlebotomy certification in my early days of college. But something about being tied up as a hostage and almost offed by a crazed killer a few months back had made me more squeamish than I'd once been.

I needed to suck it up for Charles, for Brock, and for Yo-Yo, though. They were all counting on me.

"A fresh set of eyes could help," I offered, secretly picturing the worst in my mind's eye.

Okay, time to change the subject before I had a mini freak out.

"What are we meeting Brock about today?" I asked, feigning calm.

"Normal attorney-client stuff," Charles answered rather unhelpfully. "I can introduce the two of you and let him know how you helped to get the news story delayed, but I really don't have anything else to tell him at this point."

"Then why go? Why not call with a quick update?"

Charles sighed and tightened his grip on the

steering wheel. "I'm hoping he might have some-thing new to tell me, something to help with the defense."

I sighed, too. While I was happy for the chance to meet Brock and decide for myself whether I believed he did it, I doubted he'd suddenly remember the one detail that could save him after weeks of sitting in prison. Charles didn't need to hear me express my doubts, though. I was sure he had his own.

It also seemed I'd recently become the unofficial case optimist. If I started acting defeated now, we wouldn't stand a chance of securing an innocent ruling.

When we arrived outside the state prison, I was surprised by how small and unassuming it appeared from the outside. Maybe I was expecting a giant, sprawling facility containing watchtower turrets with snipers and barbed wire fencing that stretched two stories high, but that definitely wasn't what I got. The concrete-faced building looked like something you might spot in a strip mall—not like a secure detention center for nearly a thousand inmates accused of everything from drug posses-sion to murder.

"You going to be okay?" Charles asked, pulling

the car into the visitors' parking lot.

"I'm fine." I unbuckled my seat belt with shaky hands while keeping my eyes focused straight ahead. "Let's get this over with."

The inside of the prison felt much closer to what I'd expected—the guards, the metal detectors, the holding cells. Frankly, the whole scene gave me the creeps. I followed Charles wordlessly as we were guided into one of the private attorney-client rooms. Once there, we had to wait several minutes before Brock was brought out to join us.

There, our client stood with shackles securing his hands and feet and an unbecoming beige uniform that washed out his light complexion. His dark hair appeared overgrown and poorly washed. His gray eyes were deep-set, with heavy circles painted beneath them.

When he saw us waiting for him, he smiled and ducked his head politely. Even though he was easily six foot four and had sizeable muscles to round out his physique, he seemed so small standing there before us. And then I felt it, that same gut feeling I'd teased Charles about just one day earlier. It was as if a thunder bolt of understanding struck me in my very core.

Boom!

Just like that, I knew for sure that Brock Calhoun didn't belong in this awful place and that he couldn't possibly have murdered those people.

Brock turned toward me askance, waiting for an introduction perhaps. He smiled hesitantly, politely, un-killer-ly.

"Hi, Brock," I said after clearing my throat. "My name's Angie, and I'm going to help win your case."

7

ust as I feared, Brock had nothing new to share with us during our visit. That meant it was up to me, Charles, and the pets to find a new angle for his defense—and finding a new angle meant finding the real murderer.

Was I scared? Oh, yeah.

Last time I'd gone head-to-head with a killer I almost ended up dead myself. For now, I'd try my best not to think about that. When all this was over, though, I'd definitely be booking some therapy sessions.

Back at the office, Charles handed me a thick folder filled past bursting with the prosecution's discovery, all the facts and files they believed would prove Brock guilty of the Hayes's murders.

"Wow," I said, letting out a low whistle as I flipped through the many, many pages it contained. "They sure have a lot."

Charles groaned and slumped into the chair beside me. "Yeah, they really do."

I only looked at the crime scene photos for a few seconds before pushing them aside. The gruesome pictures showed that poor Bill and Ruth had not died a gentle death. The deep crimson puddles of blood that pooled around their heads made my stomach churn.

Who would do such a horrible thing? And, perhaps even more importantly, *why?*

Charles returned to his desk for a moment. When he came back to our shared workspace, he placed a much thinner folder on the table before me. "Our discovery," he said.

"Oh." He had a few prior cases and character witnesses for Brock, but not much else to go by. It definitely didn't look good. "Who gave these statements?" I asked, holding up the character testimonies.

Charles grabbed the thin bunch of papers and described each one as he placed them back before me. "His sister, a few previous clients of his handyman business, an old girlfriend."

"Have you talked to anyone who knew the victims?"

He shook his head. "Just Brock and his sister."

"What about the witnesses for the prosecution?" I asked, returning to the thick discovery folder and pulling out several pages of testimony from inside.

Charles didn't even bother reaching for these papers. Instead he shrugged and explained, "They prefer not to talk to our side pre-trial."

"Well, that's convenient," I grumbled, blowing out a big puff of air that ruffled my bangs.

No one seemed to be playing fair here—nobody except for Charles, that was. And this fact put us at a huge disadvantage.

Charles could take the high road all he wanted. I knew perfectly well that sometimes back roads were the only way to reach your destination, and I was definitely not opposed to taking them. "Okay, so hear me out on this… What if they don't know they're talking to us?" I suggested with a sly grin.

He crossed his arms and shook his head. "Everyone knows I'm the attorney on Brock's case. Even if I wanted to be sneaky, I couldn't. And, no, I don't want to be sneaky. I want to win this case and clear Brock's name fair and square."

"Oh, sure. I understand," I acquiesced quickly. "Forget I said anything."

Charles and I spent the next several hours reviewing both sets of discovery and planning our cross-examination of the witnesses. He didn't need to know that I'd secretly made a list of people to visit outside of office hours. No one would recognize me as being part of the case.

After all, few people ever paid any real attention to paralegals.

I could use that to my advantage to learn more about the victims and figure out who might have wanted them dead. Nothing needed to come out in court unless I found our smoking gun—or, in this particular case, our bloody hammer.

* * *

"Are you ready, Nan?" I asked when I showed up to collect her for our after-hours private investigation. Because I'd arrived at work early that day, I was also able to sneak out a bit early. This gave us just enough time to stop by Bill Hayes's former place of employment and see what new information we could learn about him and any potential murder suspects that might be lurking around his office.

"Oh, yeah," Nan drawled with a vaguely Southern accent. "Let's do this."

Have I mentioned that my grandmother used to be a huge star on Broadway? She acted in the occasional community theater production now, but still jumped at any opportunity to dust off her underutilized talents. That's why I'd invited her to tag along with me tonight.

The late Mr. Hayes had worked at a place called Bayside Printing Company. Most of their jobs involved printing promotional materials for the many businesses scattered across Blueberry Bay, but a quick search on their website informed us that they also helped independent authors and micropresses publish their books. This gave us the perfect excuse to stop in for a chat.

You see, for years, Nan had been telling anyone who would listen that she had a book in her—and more specifically, an autobiography. She'd even decided upon a title despite the fact she had yet to write a single page.

"It's called *From Broadway to Blueberry Bay: The Life and Times of Dorothy Loretta Lee*, and I guarantee it's the most fabulous piece of printing that will ever come across your desk," she told the printing manager with a big jazz hands finish.

I studied the unassuming middle-aged man sitting across from us. His name was Mr. Weber, and with his thinning hairline and well-ironed shirt tucked neatly into his pants, he definitely didn't look like a murderer. He smiled at Nan with genuine interest as she regaled him with all the stories of her fake youth growing up in the South.

"It truly sounds fascinating," he said, mirroring her accent.

I had to fight hard not to crack up laughing at them both as they spoke chummily in their matching set of fake accents.

"Let me run some numbers so we can get settled on a quote," he said as he made a big show of pulling his keyboard toward him on the desk.

"Lovely," Nan said, folding her hands in her lap.

Mr. Weber's smile didn't leave his face as he clicked a series of boxes on his computer screen, pausing occasionally to ask Nan questions like how many pages her book would contain, what trim size she needed, if she wanted cream or white paper, paperback or hardcover.

Nan didn't hesitate one bit as she flawlessly trotted out each response to Mr. Weber's apparent satisfaction. It made me wonder if perhaps she was really serious about this autobiography despite the fact she hadn't yet begun to write it.

Well, I would just have to make the time to figure out how I could be more supportive of her dream later. Right now, the investigation needed my full attention.

"*So...*" I said, drawing out the syllable until Mr. Weber turned his attention to me. "Isn't this the place where that poor Bill Hayes worked before he was so tragically murdered?"

Mr. Weber turned red and sweat began to bead on his forehead at the mere mention of the victim's name. "Yes," he said with poorly concealed rage. "No one deserves to be killed like that, but especially not Bill."

"Such a terrible thing that happened," Nan said, patting his hand and offering a sympathetic nod.

A calm washed over Mr. Weber following Nan's touch. "Bill was the best employee I had and was even poised to take over for me when I retire next year," he explained with a frown. "I guess that won't be happening now."

"That's too bad," Nan said while I silently thanked my lucky stars that I'd decided to bring her with me. "I can tell you work very hard. You deserve a break after so many years of devoting yourself to the company."

He shook his head sadly. "Bill was the very same. Everyone in the office loved him. All the customers, too. There were so many times a client would come to us with a crazy rush deadline, and Bill wouldn't even think twice before offering to stay late and put in extra hours to make sure they got their order on time."

"It sounds like he was a wonderful asset to Bayside Printing Company," I added with a reassuring nod, not wanting to be completely outdone by Nan.

Mr. Weber kept his eyes glued to Nan, though, as he sighed and said, "I still can't wrap my head around it. What did that handyman have against Bill? And to kill his wife, too? I hope they put him away for a long, long time."

I shifted in my seat uncomfortably as Mr. Weber forced a smile back on his face and turned his computer monitor toward us.

"Anyway," he said after clearing his throat twice. "As you can see, you're looking at a cost of $2,500 to $6,700, depending on how many copies you'd like to print for your first run."

Nan nodded. "What would you rec—?"

Suddenly, she broke into a terrible coughing fit, unable to speak another word as she clutched at her chest dramatically.

"Excuse me," she croaked out once the coughs had subsided. "Mr. Weber, would it be possible for me to have a cup of water?"

He popped to his feet quicker than I might have expected a man of his girth and stature to be able. "Sure, that's no problem at all. Excuse me. I'll be right back."

As soon as he'd rushed out of the office, Nan began rummaging through the papers on his desk and snapping bursts of pictures with her cell phone camera.

"What are you doing?" I whispered.

Nan didn't pause as she ground out her answer. "Seeing if we can find anything he's not telling us. When he comes back with my water, excuse yourself to use the bathroom and see if you can find anything in the main office."

Wow, my nan made an excellent private investigator. Perhaps I'd have to include her on my cases more often. Then again, this was only my second case to date and already she'd proved indispensable to both. Hey, I'd take help wherever and from whomever I could get it, just so long as nothing I did ever put my dear nan in any danger.

When heavy footsteps clopped their way back down the hall, Nan slipped her phone back into her purse just in time to greet Mr. Weber with a gracious smile. "My hero," she cooed as he handed her the cup of water.

"If you'll excuse me," I said, rising to my feet. "I just need to use the bathroom real quick."

"Turn left, then it's the second door on the right," Mr. Weber muttered without looking up to see me off. He'd fallen under Nan's spell as so many did, and I couldn't fault him for that—especially since it would make my investigation that much easier.

"Thanks," I muttered before clicking the door shut behind me. Even though Nan was obviously an old pro, I myself was still new to this whole snooping business and didn't really know where I should be looking. Somehow, I doubted Bayside Printing Company would just leave their financials or security tapes in plain view. Come to think of it, a place like Bayside probably didn't even have security tapes, although if they did that would make this whole thing so much easier.

Man, I wished Octo-Cat was here with me.

Where I was gangly and untalented, my cat was an expert at sticking his nose in others' business. Heck, *snooping* might as well have been one of his middle names. With such a long list of them, it might actually be hidden in there without me knowing. He even put Nan to shame with his immense spying skills and the zero remorse he showed over exercising them. Maybe I could channel some of that now...

Now, if I were Octo-Cat, where would I look first?

I didn't get a chance to find out, because a moment later I found that I wasn't alone in the main office. The tall, slim woman who sat silently in the waiting area perked up upon noticing me.

"Can I help you?" I asked hesitantly. It seemed rude to just ignore her, even though I hadn't a clue how I could actually help her with anything of consequence.

"Is Mr. Weber in?" she asked, tucking a fluffy red curl behind her ear and offering me a friendly smile. "I was hoping to grab my order before he closed up shop for the night."

"Um, sure. I'll just go tell him you're here," I said, turning back toward the office in defeat.

I sure hoped Nan was having better luck with Mr. Weber than I'd had out here. Or that she had captured something valuable on her camera during her sleuthing micro-burst.

Otherwise, it looked like Bayside Printing Company might be a big, fat dead end. All we'd managed to do was waste valuable time.

Wednesday was almost upon us, and we weren't any closer to finding the Hayes's real killer. Might tomorrow turn out to be our lucky day?

Oh, I sure hoped so.

8

WEDNESDAY

The next morning I told Charles about the reconnaissance Nan and I had attempted at the Bayside Printing Company the night before.

"I knew you were up to something," he said before widening his eyes and asking, "Did you find anything that can help?"

I caught him up on the little things we'd learned, like that Bill was well-liked at his job and slated for a promotion the following year. In the end, we really hadn't gained anything more than that. Most of Nan's pictures had turned out blurry, and the few we could see clearly showed nothing useful.

I tapped my pen on the desk and chewed my

lower lip. "Are you sure that none of the prosecution's witnesses would be willing to talk to us before the trial?"

"I'm sure," Charles answered with a weary sigh. "They all said *no*. Well, except for one, but I haven't been able to get a hold of her despite trying to call multiple times." He shrugged and took a sip from his coffee cup before adding, "I'm not sure she'll be taking the stand, anyway."

"Oh? Who might that be?" I leaned in closer, eager to hear more. Had Charles been sitting on this lead the whole time? I wished he would have said something earlier.

He didn't seem to think it was a big deal as he casually informed me, "Michelle Hayes, the daughter."

My heart quickened at this revelation. Could Michelle be the missing key to unlock the perfect defense?

"Don't get so excited," Charles warned me. "I'm telling you, she's all but impossible to get a hold of."

"Just like this case is impossible to defend?" I quipped, shooting him a wry grin. Suddenly, a dark thought occurred to me. "You don't think she's not returning your calls because *she* did it, do you?"

"Absolutely no way. She loved her parents. They

were paying *beaucoup* bucks to put her through private college, and she still came home almost every weekend to visit even though her school is a good three-hour drive from here."

"I thought you couldn't get a hold of her?" I asked suspiciously. He seemed awfully quick to jump to Michelle's defense. Was it possible he wasn't sharing everything he knew with me? And, if so, why?

Charles seemed unperturbed by my question, and he held his coffee firmly between both hands as he said, "That was in the statement she gave the police."

"What's her number?" I asked, crossing the office to grab his landline. This week, Derek had graciously agreed to switch workspaces with me so that Charles and I could have unfettered access to each other while I assisted on Brock's case. It definitely made things easier.

Until Charles yanked the phone right out of my hand.

"It's way too early in the morning to be calling a nineteen-year-old student. You think she's going to want to talk to us if we wake her from a dead sleep?"

I cringed at his choice of words, but ultimately agreed. "Later then."

"Do you think we could try the animals again today?" Charles asked with a similar puppy dog expression to the one I'd seen on Yo-Yo's face when we'd first met.

"Sure. Why not?" I answered. We had to do something. Maybe I could put in a call to Michelle when he wasn't paying attention.

"Okay," Charles said before letting a relieved whoosh of air escape from his lungs. "Let's go."

"Not so fast," I called after him.

He'd already grabbed his things and made it halfway out the door. Talk about eager. Charles turned back to me, properly chastised. "What's wrong?"

"We need a plan first." I returned to my seat and flipped to a new page on my bright yellow legal pad.

Charles sat back down, too, but began to bounce both legs nervously.

When I was sure I had his attention, I continued, "We need to treat the animals just like we would any other witness, and we need to approach Yo-Yo as a vulnerable witness. You saw the trauma he went through at the mere suggestion his owners might be hurt. We can't upset him like that again or he may close off to us completely. Also, if we push too hard, I worry it could negatively impact his long-term mental health."

Charles thought about this for a moment. By the time he spoke again, his nervous bouncing had ceased. "Do you think Yo-Yo saw the murder?"

"He definitely could have seen it," I said with a nod.

Understanding sparked within his pine-colored eyes. "He saw it, and then he suppressed the memory to protect himself."

"That's what I'm thinking." I brought the pen to my mouth but stopped short before I began to gnaw at the cap. It was a nervous habit of mine—a disgusting habit—I definitely didn't want to trot out in front of Charles.

Luckily, he didn't seem to notice. "So how do we get him to acknowledge these hidden memories in time to save Brock?"

"We don't," I said, recapping the pen and placing it back onto the desk. "I think Yo-Yo can still help even without remembering what happened or knowing that his owners were killed. I mean, who knows a person better than their dog? He saw their daily routines for years. He would definitely know if anything had changed shortly before their deaths."

"Smart," Charles said with a nod while my heart secretly swelled at the compliment. "Do you want to take the lead on the questioning?"

"Yes, I think I do." I could talk to animals for a reason. At first I thought helping Octo-Cat solve Ethel's murder had just been a fluke, but more and more it seemed like this was my calling: to uncover justice one fluffy critter at a time.

* * *

A couple hours later, we'd prepared an exhaustive list of questions and prompts, and even role-played how a conversation with Yo-Yo might go. That only left one variable for which we hadn't properly accounted—Octo-Cat.

His mood changed so regularly, it would take far too long to draw out the various scenarios we might be faced with while trying to secure his compliance. Also, I was too embarrassed to admit to Charles how much I let my cat walk all over me on a daily basis. Instead, we planned to just show up at my house and tell Octo-Cat what we expected of him, plain and simple.

Oh, he'd definitely find a way to punish me for it, but I could handle a little cat puke or a fresh claw wound if it meant saving an innocent man from a life in prison and protecting a sweet terrier's innocence.

We stopped off at Cliffside Apartments to grab Yo-Yo, then made a quick detour to the pet store where we purchased a leash and harness for Octo-Cat. Unfortunately, the only get-up they had in his size was bright neon green with a series of fluorescent bones patterned along the leash.

This would make it that much harder to convince him to wear it, but we didn't have time to stop off at multiple stores just to assuage my cat's vanity.

Sure enough, Octo-Cat baulked when presented with his shiny new walking gear. "So let me get this straight. You not only want me to spend more time talking to Dum-Dum while you make heart eyes at Upchuck, but you also expect me to wear this monstrosity? *Ma'am, I am a cat,* not some common, mouth-breathing dog."

I crossed my legs and sat down on the floor in front of him, arranging my face in the best approximation of puppy-dog eyes any human could hope to muster. *"Please.* It's just for a little while, and I wouldn't ask unless it was really important."

He flicked his tail a few times before responding with, "So you're asking then? That means I have a choice. I choose *no."*

I gave Charles the signal we had discussed, knowing in advance that it would most likely prove necessary. I watched as he slowly slipped his hands into a pair of oven mitts and tiptoed toward Octo-Cat from behind.

"I want you to know..." I told my soon-to-be furious furr-enemy. "I was hoping it wouldn't come to this."

Octo-Cat's eyes widened with the knowledge of my betrayal at the same time I shouted, *"Now!"*

A furious cry ripped through the house as Charles scooped my cat into his arms, clutching him tightly and very much against his will.

"Unhand me, Upchuck!" he screamed as he swiped his claws in any and every direction. "I will not be disrespected like this!"

"Shh," I said in a futile attempt to coax him into a belated agreement as I worked his arms through the harness. "You do this for me, help us find who killed Yo-Yo's owners, and I will owe you a favor. It

can be any favor you want. I swear. Please just help us. We need you. And, if you'll recall, it wasn't so long ago I risked my life to help you get justice for Ethel."

At these words, all the fight drained from his furry little body, and Octo-Cat sighed heavily. "Fine," he growled as I clipped the harness under his belly.

Charles set him back on the ground, and Octo-Cat took a few tipsy steps. His fur stuck out in various directions from the struggle, and he twitched spasmodically while keeping his posture low and defensive.

"You owe me a big favor," he shouted in my direction. "The biggest favor you've ever given anyone in all your nine lives!"

I nodded, eager to put this confrontation to an end. I'd braced myself for a much bigger fight than he'd given me, and things could still go south if I wasn't careful. "You've got it," I promised. "Anything."

Octo-Cat let out a maniacal chuckle that made the small hairs on the back of my neck stand on end, too.

"What?" I asked, my voice suddenly shaky and unsure.

"Oh, you'll see. You'll all see!" He swept a paw toward Charles, which only increased my worry—but my crazy cat's demands could be dealt with later. Thinking of which, I should also probably put parent controls on the TV later to discourage this kind of crazed villainous behavior. Right now, though, we had to move on to the next phase of our plan, just in case he suddenly changed his mind and retracted his offer to help.

"Let's get out of here while we still can," I told Charles while bending down to clip the leash to Octo-Cat's new harness.

"Fully unnecessary," the tabby grumbled. "What makes you assume I'd run away? Remember, I chose you despite your many, *many* shortcomings."

"It's more for your safety than your compliance," I explained.

Even if Octo-Cat fully intended to stick with us on this trip, he had a tendency to become a different cat from the moment he stepped paw outside. Inside the house, he was a cool intellectual who freely offered an unsolicited running commentary on my life. Once he got out into the wide open, though, he became flighty, unpredictable, and highly excitable. For all I knew, he could spot a butterfly and run three miles straight before realizing we weren't right there chasing it with him.

Yes, as annoying as he could sometimes be, I loved my cat and wanted to keep him with me for many years to come.

Unfortunately for him, that meant he needed to wear the harness.

I only hoped the favor he requested of me would be something I could legally and physically obtain for him. You just never knew with this guy. That's part of what made living with him so exciting most days.

Then there were days like today…

I knew the worst of his agitation was yet to come.

Grabbing a thick, long-sleeved jacket from the closet, I took a deep breath and led our motley party toward Charles's waiting car.

It was time for phase two.

9

We arrived in the Hayes's old neighborhood less than ten minutes later, and Yo-Yo immediately perked up upon taking in the familiar sights and smells. He barked, howled, whimpered, and whined, all before we even managed to find a place to park the car.

"What's he saying?" I asked Octo-Cat, who sat velcroed to my lap in the passenger seat. Since I wasn't driving this time, I'd had the blessedly bright idea to bring a cushion to place between his claws and me. Never before had I enjoyed such a nice car ride with my agoraphobic cat.

Octo-Cat, of course, was still less than thrilled to be in the moving vehicle. It took a few moments before he answered. "He's calling out to his mom and dad and letting them know he's come home," he explained between nervous pants.

"Oh, that's really sad," I responded after offering a quick translation for Charles. Despite the obvious seriousness of the situation, speaking to each other like this reminded me of the old schoolyard game of telephone. How warped did Yo-Yo's words become by the time they finally reached Charles?

"Definitely a vulnerable witness," Charles agreed with my earlier assessment while pulling up to the curb and putting the car in park. "Poor guy."

"You still haven't told me the plan," Octo-Cat said as I helped him untangle his claws from the cushion and placed him gently on the pavement outside.

Charles grabbed Yo-Yo's leash and came around the car to stand beside us. The excited terrier strained so hard against his leash, he began to wheeze.

"Yup. Dum-Dum is definitely a much better name for this dog," Octo-Cat said with a contented grin, clearly feeling like himself again now that he was back on solid ground. "Upchuck suits the human, too."

"Yes, yes, you're a great nicknamer," I said to placate him, resisting the urge to roll my eyes now that he knew what the gesture meant. Instead, I chose to answer his earlier question. "The plan is to walk around the neighborhood and see what Yo-Yo can tell us about his life before. Something he says could give us a clue as to who besides Brock might have committed the murder."

"Wouldn't it be easier if you just told Dum-Dum the truth about what happened and asked him to help?" Octo-Cat almost seemed as if he was trying to help, but I suspected the real goal was to end his involvement with our case as soon as felinely possible.

"No!" I shouted at the same time Yo-Yo screeched and began to twist at the end of the leash. Any passerby would have thought we were torturing the poor Yorkie. Thankfully, we had the street to ourselves for the moment.

"Dum-Dum says he wants to know the truth," Octo-Cat explained with a bored expression and a yawn.

"Ugh, stop making things harder than they have to be," I scolded him. "And stop being such an elitist. His name is Yo-Yo, and you know it."

"Yes, I'm the one making things harder here," my cat said, widening his eyes in the direction of the neon-colored leash that tied me and him together. He let out an exasperated huff and looked away.

I'd had more than enough of his complaints, especially since Yo-Yo was still panicking—and doing so loudly. Dropping to my haunches, I stared the obstinate tabby down and said, "If you want your return favor, you'll do things the way I want them done. You hear?"

He cringed. "Say it. Don't spray it. And you don't have to shout, either."

Okay, that was it. I would definitely be restricting his TV access. It was bad enough when he was watching educational cartoons all hours of the day, but now he'd turned into a snarky teenager—and that was just too much when combined with his already snarky feline temperament. Besides, he needed to learn that his actions had consequences.

Ugh. Here I was still in my twenties and yet somehow also a single mother to a whiny teenager. I owed Nan and my parents a huge apology for all the irritating know-it-all things I'd done as a teenage brat myself.

"Are we agreed?" I asked pointedly as I stood up and Charles bent down to pick up Yo-Yo so that he would stop hurting himself.

"Fine," Octo-Cat spat out. "What do you want me to tell him?"

I put on a huge smile to show Octo-Cat how pleased I was about his cooperation. I knew better than to call him a good boy in front of mixed company, even though he loved hearing those words when it was just the two of us at home. "Tell him his mom and dad are away on a trip right now, but we're going to take a walk around his neighborhood together because we'd love to hear about all his favorite memories with them."

"You do realize this is going to be torture for me, right?"

"You'll live," I shot back.

Octo-Cat conveyed my message to Yo-Yo, who briefly stopped panting and slipped his tongue back inside his mouth. A few seconds later, his enthusiasm returned, and he struggled to break free of Charles's grasp once more.

"Ready?" Charles asked.

When I nodded, he placed the terrier on the ground, and the four of us began our walk around the neighborhood with Yo-Yo proudly leading the way.

"Do I have to translate everything he says?" Octo-Cat whined less than a minute into our jaunt.

"Yes, everything," I answered.

Charles stayed oddly silent as the animals and I conversed. On the rare occasion we ran into another walker, he spoke, too, so that I would appear at least somewhat less insane. I was still walking a very angry-looking cat on a leash, after all.

"Careful, he bites," Charles warned a pair of blue-haired ladies in track suits when it looked like they were going to try to pet Octo-Cat.

Octo-Cat hissed and arched his back for good measure, then laughed when they quickened their pace and power-walked right on by us. "That was kind of fun," he said as he shook it out.

"Awesome, so glad you're enjoying yourself. Now, what is Yo-Yo saying?" I demanded. I was glad Octo-Cat had found a way to make the experience more palatable, but we needed him to stay focused on the entire reason for this trip in the first place.

The tabby sighed and twitched his whiskers and moved his ears back and forth. "Let me just turn on my Dum-Dum receptors... *There.*"

"Haha, you're hilarious. Now stop with the stand-up comedy and start with the translation already."

"*Fiiiiiiiine,*" he drew that single word out for at

least seven syllables before finally doing as he was told. He sighed and said, "Well, that rock we just passed a few paces back, that's one of his favorite places to pee. Once he saw a squirrel crossing the road here, and it ran so fast he couldn't catch up. Birds like to sit in that tree over there. He also enjoys peeing there. There's usually a nest every spring. The kids who live in that house up ahead like to run through the sprinklers in summer, and sometimes they invite him to play…"

I was starting to get his hesitation about translating *everything* Yo-Yo said. It all came out so fast there was no way I could relay it to Charles. I offered him an apologetic glance before asking Octo-Cat, "Do you think you could ask him some questions for me?"

He just kept walking without so much as looking at me.

I took his silence as agreement. "Ask him if he likes all the people who live in this neighborhood."

"He says, 'yes, very much,' then he told about the time he saw two red cars in a row right on this block."

I needed to keep both of them talking, but I also needed to keep them on topic. "Were Bill and Ruth particularly close to anyone in the area?"

"Apparently they liked everybody, and everybody liked them," Octo-Cat relayed. I was beginning to wonder if our terrier friend might not be the most reliable of witnesses. It seemed he saw the best in everybody—and every situation, too.

"Anything yet?" Charles asked.

I shook my head and kicked at a pebble in our path. "No. Unless you count knowing all the best places to mark your territory along this block."

Charles laughed, but I could tell he was at least a little—and probably *a lot*—disappointed. I was just about to suggest we head back when Yo-Yo barked defensively. He stopped walking and grew stiff, pointing his nose to the next yard over.

"What is it?" I asked my cat as excitement surged through my veins.

"He says that's the bad lady. He wants her to go away."

I followed Yo-Yo's gaze to the "For Sale" sign down the block. There, a blue and white notice announced that the property was being sold through Calhoun Realty, and a picture of Brock smiling beside his twin sister, Breanne, graced its countenance.

"Lady, right?" I asked carefully. "Not man?"

"Definitely lady," Octo-Cat concurred. "He said

that she always shoved him into a closet whenever people came to visit and that made him sad and scared."

"Hmm, I wonder if that could be the same closet that Bill and Ruth's bodies were found inside."

Octo-Cat took a deep breath and turned toward Yo-Yo.

"*Don't translate that!"* I shouted.

"What are they saying?" Charles nudged my arm while wearing an expression of utter glee. "Do we have a lead?"

I glanced from the sign to Yo-Yo and then to Charles. "Well, the dog that likes everyone has a very negative impression of Breanne Calhoun. It seems we might need to pay her a little visit."

* * *

As we walked back toward the car, Charles placed a call to Breanne —or at least he tried to get through to her.

"Straight to voicemail," he said with a frustrated groan.

"Text her?" I suggested.

Charles did, and we heard back from her almost

right away. He handed me the phone, so I could read the message for myself:

Showing houses to a client. Everything okay?

I gave the phone back to Charles, who deftly composed his reply while speaking each word aloud to keep me in the loop. "Can we meet about the case?"

A quick series of pings followed, and Charles relayed, "She can't tonight, but says we can stop in tomorrow any time after lunch."

"Great," I moaned. Tomorrow would be Thursday, and my mom's story was set to run Friday. That sure didn't leave us much time, especially if Breanne turned out to be yet another false lead.

"So what now?" I asked.

"I'm kind of hungry," Charles answered. "Do you know of any place we can get a good lobster roll? I've been craving one ever since I moved here."

I stopped dead in my tracks. "Are you serious right now, Charles Longfellow, the Third?"

"What? What did I do?"

"You've been in Maine how long and haven't had one of our famous lobster rolls?"

He laughed. "Have I mentioned I'm kind of a workaholic?"

"This won't fly, Chuck," I said, finally feeling

comfortable using his nickname. "Since you've waited this long, not just any lobster roll will do. You need the best."

"I'm definitely okay with that. Which place has the best?"

"C'mon, we're headed to Misty Harbor and a little place called the Little Dog Diner. I just know you're going to love it."

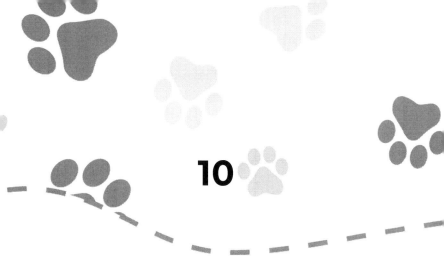

10

Our dinner detour in the nearby town of Misty Harbor proved to be just the thing both Charles and I needed to ease our frazzled nerves. Of course, we'd stopped by my house to drop off Octo-Cat along the way—a fact for which he was exceedingly grateful—but we brought Yo-Yo with us and dined at one of their outdoor tables that looked right onto the bay. We even got the pup a fish dinner of his own, which he devoured with aplomb. I saved a small portion in a to-go box for Octo-Cat as a thank you for his help that day, and also with the hope he'd go easy on me whenever he revealed the favor I'd need to grant him in return.

Charles and I sat and chatted over lobster rolls

until the sky began to darken and another restaurant-goer needed our table. I thought I recognized the woman with red, fluffy hair, who approached us with a smile and a request to take over our spot, but I couldn't quite place her. Anyway, it looked like she was busy, because the moment we gathered our things to leave, she plopped down and unpacked a laptop from her bag. That was before the busboy had even managed to clear away our plates.

I felt bad for her, having no one to dine with her on this beautiful Wednesday night, even though I'd be home in my jammies fighting with Octo-Cat by now if it weren't for this impromptu outing with Charles.

"See," he said, bumping my shoulder with his own. "At least I know not to mix work and lobster rolls."

Work, ugh. Yes, our momentary break from the case had come to an end. There wasn't much time left now.

"Can we try calling Michelle now?" I suggested as we made our way back to the parking lot.

"Sure, use my phone," he said. "I have her number saved just in case."

I tried my luck but got sent straight to voicemail where a robotic voice informed me the mailbox was full and thus unable to take any new messages. "So much for that," I said with a defeated sigh.

"Hey. At least tomorrow's a new day," Charles told me with a wistful glance in my direction.

Yes, a new day—and the last full one we had when it came to proving Brock's innocence and stopping my mom's big exposé. Even with the animals' help, this was not turning out as easy as I'd hoped.

Could we possibly hope that a new day would make that any different?

THURSDAY

Charles and I put in a full morning at the firm before heading over to Calhoun Realty around noon. He'd practically insisted we bring the animals with us, but fortunately I was able to convince him that we should meet with Breanne on our own before getting Octo-Cat and Yo-Yo involved—especially since we had no idea how the little dog would react to seeing Breanne in person. If she was our killer, all heck could break lose once Yo-Yo's memories came rushing back. And, judging by his reaction to seeing her printed image yesterday, that was a very real possibility.

We had to wait more than half an hour before Breanne ushered us back into her office. Even though I was sure she was a very busy person, this immediately soured her to me. One of my biggest pet peeves was people who didn't respect others' time. Didn't she know her brother's freedom was on the line here?

"Sorry about that," the realtor said when at last she waved us back into her private office. Of course, she didn't seem the least bit apologetic despite her words to the contrary.

Charles and I sat in the matching pair of chairs in front of her desk and waited for Breanne to settle herself. She seemed rather put out by our arrival even though she'd known we were coming.

"How is everything?" Charles asked, putting on the same drawn expression I'd seen him use when speaking with Brock at the prison.

"Not so hot," she admitted, tossing her auburn hair into a messy bun at the nape of her neck. With her hair pulled back, I noticed how strongly she resembled her brother. I guess that made sense, them being twins and all, but still I found the simi-larity quite striking and a bit shocking. The only differences seemed to be the feminine curve to Breanne's face and the alternate hair color.

She pinched her features in dismay before jumping into a lengthy explanation. "Half the people I take out on showings don't even want a house. They just want to gossip about my brother. Or, worse, sometimes they want to chew me out on his behalf. Still, I'm taking as many extra hours as I can, because your firm doesn't come cheap. And, if Brock is convicted, I can pretty much kiss this realty goodbye." Breanne laughed sarcastically and let out a long sigh. "So, yeah, not so hot."

"I'm sorry to be intruding on your busy schedule," Charles said. He didn't seem too apologetic, either. "But we need to explore every possible lead that comes before us, and your brother has asked that I keep you informed of all new developments for his case."

I shifted uncomfortably in my chair as I tried my best not to stare at her with open hostility. If there was one thing the past few months had taught me, it was that I could trust what animals said far more than I could trust humans. For all we knew, Breanne might just be playing the part of the aggrieved sister, all the while framing her poor brother for a crime she committed.

The most convincing evidence I had to support my theory, of course, was the fact that the happy-go-lucky Yorkie who loved everyone became insecure and defensive when confronted with a mere picture of her.

What else could something like that mean?

I did wish Charles would've been open to the idea of having Nan accompany us. She could have engaged in some of her grade-A sleuthing while Charles and I spoke directly to Breanne. I'd only met this realtor minutes ago and already knew better than to trust a single word that came out of her glossy red mouth.

"Has there been a new development?" Breanne asked, crossing her legs above the knee and staring Charles down. "Go on, tell me about it, then."

Charles glanced toward me and took a deep breath. Oh, gosh, I hope he wasn't planning on telling her about the talking animals or that we now suspected her because of them.

"This is Angie Russo," he said as he gestured toward me.

I smiled and waggled my fingers at her awkwardly.

"She's Blueberry Bay's best paralegal and has

recently signed on to help me defend your brother's case."

"That's all well and good," Breanne said with a disappointed shake of her head. "But I hired a lawyer, not a paralegal. With as much as we're paying, Mr. Thompson should really be defending this case himself. Please tell me you didn't request this meeting just to tell me you have a new assistant. That is not news I should have to pay $275 an hour to hear!"

"Don't worry. This visit is off the clock," Charles said with an ingratiating smile. Somehow it actually seemed to work, too.

"Oh?" the pretty realtor said, sitting a little higher in her chair. "Then how can I help you today?"

"In reviewing the discovery with Angie here, we came up with a few new questions regarding the crime scene. Would it be possible for us to have another look around this afternoon?"

"You want to see the house again," she said flatly. "I guess that's fine."

"Great, thank you so much." Charles rose to his feet and extended a hand across the desk. "If you could just give us the key then, we'll be on our way."

"Not so fast," Breanne said as she stood up with him. "The State Licensing Board is already watching me like a hawk. Even if Brock gets off the hook, the fact still remains that the killer could have gained access to the Hayes's home through my lockbox. Someone even suggested that maybe I didn't close it up properly and that's why my clients were murdered. Can you believe that?"

"Tough break," I muttered. Apparently, this was the wrong thing to say.

Breanne's eyes narrowed in on me and she pinched her lips together in quiet contemplation before shifting her gaze back to Charles. "What did you say her name was again?"

"Angie Russo," I answered on my own behalf, purposefully not offering to shake hands on our re-introduction. "Now can we please go see the house?"

Her eyes zipped back to mine, and this time she sneered openly. The two of us stared at each other for a few moments before Breanne finally caved and showed us out of her office.

"We'll meet you at the house in about fifteen minutes," Charles said. "We have a quick pit stop to make first."

"Fine, but please don't be longer than that. I

have a lot of paperwork to get through tonight and would prefer not to be up all night."

I didn't say anything until Charles and I were buckled safely back inside his car. "Well, isn't she a peach?" I scoffed.

Charles appeared thoughtful as he watched Breanne pull away in her large cherry red SUV. "She's under a lot of pressure these days. Maybe even worse than her brother," he explained. His expression became almost tender, which made me feel queasy.

"But that doesn't mean she needs to be rude," I argued. "What's your plan for checking out the house, anyway? I thought the whole point of this visit was to find out if Breanne framed her brother for the murders."

"We can't exactly come right out and ask a client if she's guilty, especially since she's not the one we've been hired to defend. I figured we could grab the animals, grab the discovery, and check the place out. After all, you haven't seen the crime scene yet. You might notice something I haven't. Yo-Yo might remember something once we get him back inside."

"Yesterday, Yo-Yo seemed pretty convinced that

Breanne was to blame. He even called her 'the bad lady,'" I reminded him.

Charles kept his eyes straight ahead as if gathering his private thoughts, ones he wasn't quite ready to share with me. "Yeah, well, I know Breanne better than you, and I still don't think she did it."

"And I do," I shot back, crossing my arms over my chest like an angry toddler. If I didn't feel threatened by Breanne before, I definitely did now that Charles was going out of his way to defend her despite our evidence against her. It seemed maybe my crush had a little crush of his own.

Maybe Octo-Cat was right. Maybe I needed to find a nice cat person to settle down with and leave pining for Chuck in my past.

But then he smiled a full-on toothy grin, grabbed my hand, and gave it a good squeeze. "Only one way to find out. Let's go."

My breathing hitched in my chest. Oh, yes, I was ready to follow him anywhere. Not just because he was handsome, but also because he was smart, kind, and committed to justice.

And all of that was a good thing, too, since we were heading to the place where two people had recently been murdered...

harles and I pulled up to the Hayes's home some twenty minutes later and found Breanne waiting in her SUV idling in the driveway. When we each exited with an animal sidekick, she scrambled out and slammed the door with more strength than I thought she had in her.

Yo-Yo growled and bared his tiny incisors, but made no effort to escape Charles's arms despite either his anxiety over spending more time with a person he loathed or his unbridled joy at having finally returned home.

"What are you doing with these animals?" Breanne demanded, marching right up to us and blocking our path to the house.

Octo-Cat and I cut across the grass and let ourselves inside, leaving Charles to charm the angry realtor since neither of us would be much help there.

The moment we entered, the sharp tang of chemicals hit my nose.

Octo-Cat smelled it, too, and immediately began rubbing his paw over his face. "*Ew, ew, ew,*" he complained with each step we took further into the house. "You humans sure have a knack for fouling up your environment. I'm not sure how long I'll be able to take this."

"Me either," I said, lifting the collar of my shirt over my face to form an impromptu breathing filter. "I guess they had to give the place an extra deep cleaning after..."

Octo-Cat picked up where my words had trailed off. "The brutal murders? Yeah." His words came out muffled from beneath his paw.

I looked to him, wondering where we should go next, but the cat ignored me. Instead, he lifted his head and bravely sniffed the air, then broke into a trot and headed straight up the stairs without another second's hesitation.

"Wait," I called after him, struggling and failing to keep pace. "Where are you going?"

He didn't answer, but after climbing the stairs myself, I found him sitting in a bedroom at the end of the hallway. The large area was completely devoid of furniture, unlike the other rooms I'd passed through on my way here. It also appeared to be the source for the strong chemical smell, but otherwise the walls and carpeting appeared pristine and untouched.

I felt a little guilty stomping through the room, but that feeling left me when I managed to pry open the windows and let some fresh, non-toxic air into the space.

Octo-Cat hopped up onto the window sill appreciatively. "Now I can breathe again," he said with a contented sigh. "For a while there I thought *I* was going to die in this house, too."

I placed a hand on each hip and stared him down. "Too soon, Octo. Too soon."

He flicked his tail in agitation. "Is my punishment to lose yet another part of my name? What happened to the *Cat* in *Octo-Cat?* Hmmm?"

"I don't know," I answered truthfully, a devious smile creeping across my face. "You're giving everyone new nicknames lately, so I guess I thought I'd try it out, too. Besides, unlike you, I'm trying to lighten the mood a little bit, considering

I'm pretty sure this is the room where Bill and Ruth died."

"This is the room where they were *murdered,* you mean," Octo-Cat corrected, taking deliberate care to enunciate the terrible term. "And don't forget the *Cat* next time. It is the most important part of my name."

"Fine, but let's try to focus now. Okay? This is the place two people were killed." I dropped my voice to a whisper just in case Breanne could hear us from outside. I couldn't hear her and had no idea where she, Charles, and Yo-Yo were at the moment, so perhaps we were in good shape for now. Still, it always paid to be extra careful when letting my freak flag fly. "We need to see what we can find out while we're here and have the chance to look around."

"Yes, boss," my tabby said wryly and with another energetic flick of his tail.

A bird chirped in the tree outside the window and immediately drew his attention away. Octo-Cat slowly rose to his feet while keeping his head perfectly still, then wiggled his butt and let out a laughable impression of a bird call.

Rather than tease him, I just rolled my eyes and walked the perimeter of the room. One of us needed to get to work before this golden investigation opportunity completely passed us by. And it seemed that would have to be me.

Tucked into a little nook, I found the door to an impressive walk-in closet. This was the place the bodies had been found, although nothing—other than the chemical smell—hinted at its uncomfortably recent and gruesome history now. It was simply a plain, empty space.

"This is where they were found," Charles said, coming up behind me and causing me to jump in my skin.

"You don't just sneak up on someone in the middle of a crime scene," I hissed, turning toward him so that he could read the displeasure on my face.

His eyebrows pinched together, and his mouth drooped in a frown. Well, at least he looked properly chastised. "Sorry about that. I didn't mean to scare you, but I also worry we don't have much time. Breanne is not happy right now and even threatened to call Thompson and issue a complaint."

I shook my head and took a step back when I realized Charles and I were still standing too near each other for comfort. I had the hots for the guy, sure, but this hardly felt like the time or place. "All because we brought a couple animals with us? Does she even recognize Yo-Yo?"

Upon hearing his name, the Yorkie zipped into the room, running huge looping circles so fast, he was mostly a gray and brown blur.

"Well, someone has the zoomies," Octo-Cat declared, hopping down from the window sill and joining me and Charles by the closet. "Also he scared my bird away. I almost had it, too."

I decided not to mention that Octo-Cat also got the zoomies from time to time or that there was absolutely no way he was catching that bird—not just because his bird call was extremely unconvincing but also because of the screen window that hung between them. Add to that his whole inability to fly and we had the very definition of an impossible situation.

We watched the Yorkie run joyous circles until he collapsed in an exhausting, panting heap right in the middle of the room.

"What's going on with Breanne?" I asked Charles while Octo-Cat dutifully approached the dog and began a conversation with him.

"She says we're overstepping, and she questions our sanity." His face remained unreadable as he delivered this unwelcome news, but I could guess how he probably felt in that moment.

My heart began to gallop. It was bad enough that Charles knew my secret, but now he was telling others, too? "You didn't tell her about—"

"No," he cut me off. "But I had to tell her something, so I said they were emotional support animals."

Well, no wonder she thought we were crazy. Charles had basically confirmed that for her.

"How long do we have?" I asked, unable to resist the urge to gnaw on one of my many hangnails. I really needed to treat myself to a manicure when this whole thing was over.

"Half an hour, tops," he revealed with another deep frown.

"Then we better get to it." I approached the animals slowly and sat down beside them cross-legged. Hopefully, the chemical smell from the carpet wouldn't rub off on my clothes, but even if it did, it would be a small price to pay for information that would save Brock.

"What did he say?" I asked Octo-Cat while nodding toward our doggie eye witness.

"Lots of things. Too many things," Octo-Cat said, rolling onto his back so that his belly was facing the ceiling. He looked utterly exhausted even though he couldn't have been talking to Yo-Yo for more than two minutes before I interrupted.

"Care to tell me any of them?" I asked, resisting the urge to pet his fluffy tummy. Something told me he was already looking for a reason to bite me as an outlet for his anxiety, and neither of us needed the extra hostility right now.

He yawned, and the smell of the tuna blend breakfast on his breath mixed with the chemicals in the carpet made my stomach churn with bile. "Something about his owners and missing home. He was in the closet. They were in the closet. Yada yada yada."

"What? No *yada yada yada*. What did he say? His exact words, please." I nudged him until he rolled onto his side then forced him to look up and focus on me.

Octo-Cat growled, picked himself up, and moved a couple feet so that he was out of my reach. "I told you everything I could remember. He talks fast. And incessantly, I might add. It just all kind of runs together after a while."

Hmm, kind of like Octo-Cat himself.

I groaned, and Yo-Yo crawled onto my lap to frantically lick my face. "I cannot believe you," I told my naughty kitty. "We came here specifically to investigate the murder and you can't be bothered to pay attention for two minutes?"

"I don't need to lay here and listen to this," Octo-Cat said, pulling himself to his feet with great agitation and trotting out of the room.

Yo-Yo perked up in my lap, then hopped off to give chase.

"Well, I'm guessing we have even less time now," I told Charles, returning to my feet as well. "Where is Breanne hanging out, by the way?"

He stood in the closet studying the walls as if they were the most interesting thing in the whole world. "In her SUV," he mumbled without looking away. "She said she had some calls to make."

I swallowed the giant lump in my throat. We both knew that one of those calls might be to our boss. As much as we needed to make the most of our time here, I also needed to tread lightly as far as my boss was concerned. Mr. Fulton had always been kind and complimentary of my work, but Mr. Thompson—the only partner left at this point—made his dislike of me clear at every possible opportunity.

If Bethany was right about him planning to throw Charles under the bus when it came to this unwinnable case, I had no doubt he'd all too happily discard of me as well.

Sigh. Why were things never easy?

"Should we go after them?" I asked, pointing my chin toward the door through which the animals had just noisily departed.

Charles glanced from me to the door and back again, then shook his head. "In a little bit. First, there's something about the crime scene that's always struck me as a bit odd. Maybe you can help me figure it out." He reached into his messenger bag and pulled out the giant discovery folder from the prosecution.

Just as I feared, he flipped straight to the photos of Bill and Ruth's bloody, lifeless bodies. I hadn't wanted to see these pictures the first time, and I certainly didn't want to see them now.

But I also didn't want to see an innocent man spend the rest of his life in prison, so I grabbed some antacids from my purse, placed one on my tongue, and willed myself to examine the photos that Charles extended out to me now.

I looked closely this time. Carefully. Just as Charles had asked of me.

And wouldn't you know it? We finally found something that might actually help our case.

12

I may not have much experience with murder or crime scenes, but something about those photos jumped out at me.

"Can we lay these out in the closet?" I asked, shoving them back toward Charles.

He nodded, got down on his hands and knees, then matched the photos up to their corresponding spots in the actual physical space. Together, we spent a few minutes making sure the angles were represented perfectly.

"Okay, walk me through this," I said, rubbing my chin with the side of my index finger. "What exactly do we know from the pictures?"

Charles pointed to one on the left-hand side of our spread. "From the angle of the blood splatter, we know that the killer approached his victims from the right."

We both studied the wall, which had once been painted red with blood. Now it was a pristine and perfect white.

"Okay, what else?" I asked, chewing on a fingernail now that the antacid had fully dissolved. I needed something to ground myself in the now so my fears wouldn't get the best of me.

Charles swept his vision across the arc of photographs before turning back toward me. "Well, we believe Bill was killed first and that Ruth was killed a few minutes after when she came to investigate."

I hadn't heard this bit before, but I also hadn't asked for many details about the crime scene, either. One thing was for sure: I definitely needed to work on thickening my skin or at least strengthening my stomach when it came to these things—especially since it seemed investigating murders was becoming something of a habit for me as of late.

I nodded. "Okay. What makes you say that?"

"Bill's blood was more saturated in the carpet and spread further than Ruth's, but really it was a matter of minutes between the murders, so it's hard to say," Charles explained, keeping his voice steady. I wondered if thinking about the brutal killings upset him as much as it upset me. If it did, he certainly didn't make his feelings obvious.

"Hmm," I said, considering my investigative partner just as much as the information he'd presented. After a moment of tense silence, I grabbed a pencil from my purse and did my best to trace the area of blood splatter on the wall. Art was one of my many failed talents, but I did okay considering.

Charles panicked and tried to wrest the pencil away from me. "What are you doing?" he demanded with a look of horror on his handsome face. Although, I had to admit, he seemed less handsome today than he had at the beginning of the week. Maybe I was unconsciously beginning to associate the Hayes's double murder with him, and that definitely wasn't swoon-inducing or crush-worthy.

"Trying to match the evidence to the conclusion." I had to admit, I felt very Sherlock Holmes in that moment. Well, if Holmes had secretly harbored an on-again-off-again crush on Watson. Yeah, I still hadn't found anything groundbreaking, but something told me if we kept following this line of thought, we'd find exactly what we needed to save Brock.

My Watson unfortunately wasn't the most agreeable when it came to my current tactics. He argued, "But Breanne—"

"She's already mad," I said through gritted teeth. "It's not like this will make things any worse."

Charles sighed but moved aside and let me finish my work.

Ignoring the small droplets, I reproduced the outline for the main burst of the blood splatter carefully. A few minutes later, I stepped back, satisfied with the effort.

"Now," I said, brushing my hands off on my pants even though they hadn't gotten the slightest bit dirty. "We need to finish setting the scene. You be Bill, and I'll be the killer. Do you have anything that can work as the hammer?"

"Um..." Charles shifted his weight uncomfortably. He didn't seem to have the slightest idea what I was on about, but I didn't want to waste time explaining, especially when Breanne could barge in and disrupt us any minute.

"Never mind, we can use this." I grabbed Octo-Cat's neon leash and folded it over several times to approximate the length of a standard hammer, then tied it in place with a hair tie on each end. "Got any sticky notes in there?"

Charles fumbled around in his bag, then pulled out a mini pad of brightly colored notes, which he promptly handed to me. "Never know when these might come in handy," he said with a shrug. "In fact, I still don't know how they're going to help right now, but I'm ready to find out."

"Good," I said, eyeing him carefully for a moment. He smiled instead of grimacing, which I took as a win. "Now go lay down the way Bill was found and in the same spot, too."

He did, lowering himself gently down onto his stomach and reaching his arms overhead at odd angles. It was eerie, seeing him there sprawled out like the victim from our photos—especially since my mind automatically filled in the missing details like the blood and the giant, blossoming bruises.

I shook my head to clear my mental Etch-a-Sketch of that gruesome picture, then picked up the photo of Bill's prone body and put a series of sticky notes on Charles's back and head in the same spots where the hammer had wounded Bill. There were three in total—one near the base of his neck, one on the side of his face, and the last on his upper back near his shoulder.

"Okay. Now stand up," I instructed, taking a big step back to give him space.

Charles did without saying anything. I could tell he was intrigued and also wanted to see where this was going.

"How tall was Bill?" I asked as I motioned for my colleague to turn around so that I could study his back from behind.

"About five foot ten," he answered after a brief moment's thought.

"And how tall are you?"

"Six feet even."

"Now how tall is Brock?"

"Six-four."

I kept all these numbers in my head, adding my height of five foot seven to the mix as I brought my makeshift murder weapon up and down on each of the sticky notes. I caught each shot with the camera on my phone.

"Okay. You can turn around now." I made a quick trip to the app store to download a measuring app while I explained the next steps to Charles. "Brock is six inches taller than Bill. So now we're going to make me six inches taller than you. Can you crouch to about *yea*-high?"

I drew the phone from the floor to about my

shoulder height and held it there while Charles got into position. He was a bit shaky as I redid my measurements and snapped pictures of each.

"Now check these out with me," I said, helping him back to his feet so we could both examine the six new photos on my phone. "These first three photos are from when we were both at our normal height, and the next three are from us recreating the height difference between Bill and Brock. What do you notice?"

Charles grabbed the phone from me excitedly and flipped back and forth reviewing each photo several times, then we placed my phone onto the floor next to the crime scene photos of Bill. He looked from the walls where I'd traced the path of the blood splatter and back to the pictures.

"Given the angle of the blood splatter and placement of the wounds, the first pictures look much more accurate."

I nodded. "If Brock had landed these blows on Bill, he would have needed to angle his wrists awkwardly like this and taken a wide, golf-like swing. It would have been much more natural—and more effective—to hit him from above."

"So you think someone shorter committed the crime?"

"I do, but let's recreate Ruth's death before deciding for sure."

We went through all the same motions again, with me playing the victim this time. Ruth had only needed one blow to go down and it was directly to the top of her skull.

"See," I told Charles as we were going through the resulting photos. "Why would the murderer hit Ruth over the top of the head and not Bill?"

"Because he couldn't reach on Bill," Charles answered excitedly.

I nodded, happy to see that my companion both understood and supported my theory. "Actually, I'm pretty sure the culprit is a she. Or a very short man. In any case, it's not Brock."

"So we're looking for someone about..." His eyes found and held mine.

"My height, yup," I confirmed.

Charles grabbed the discovery folder and flipped through it quickly, mumbling the names of each witness and person of interest as he went. "It couldn't be Brock. Also couldn't be Bill's boss. Both are too tall."

I already knew exactly who this new evidence implicated, but I needed Charles to arrive there on his own.

"Almost everyone is either too tall or too short to be considered," he murmured while stashing the folder back in his bag.

"We know at least one person related to this case who's exactly my height," I pointed out.

"Breanne," Charles said with a sigh. "I was afraid of that."

A series of footsteps stomped up the staircase, causing us to share a horrified expression. We knew exactly who had come to find us now.

"Okay, time's up!" Breanne called, charging angrily into the room and growing even more livid when she found Charles and me sitting on the closet floor with the crime scene photos and a matching pair of guilty expressions on our faces.

"What are you doing?" she demanded, placing a hand on each hip. "And where are your animals?"

Uh-oh. This was not good. Not good at all.

13

bolted out of that room so fast, Breanne couldn't have stopped me if she'd tried. Maybe I was being a bit overdramatic, but I didn't feel like being trapped in the same small, enclosed space with a possible killer. Her arrival also reminded me that I hadn't heard from the animals in quite some time, and I had no idea whether they'd somehow managed to escape outside.

Luckily, I found Octo-Cat almost right away. He stood on top of the fridge with his fur puffed up and his expression angry. Yo-Yo whined and stood on his hind legs scratching the surface of the refrigerator in his desperation to reach the cat.

"Why did you abandon me?" Octo-Cat raged.

I put my hands up in surrender. "Hey, you're the

one who left in the middle of our investigation. You could have come back at any time."

"Not with Dum-Dum cornering me here," he ground out.

I knew he was irritated, but so was I. He was supposed to be finding a way to connect with our doggie witness, and that clearly had not happened.

"So, I'm guessing you did nothing useful this whole time?" I asked with a frustrated sigh.

His angry, unblinking eyes fixed right on me. "I defended my life and my dignity, and that is the most important thing of all."

I shook my head and bent down to collect Yo-Yo. "We have to go," I whispered to Octo-Cat. "And when the other humans come downstairs, I have to stop talking to you."

"What's that?" Breanne asked, appearing suddenly at the foot of the stairs. Seriously, what was it with people sneaking up on me in this house? It gave me the heebie jeebies big time.

"Just telling them it's time to go," I answered truthfully.

Charles joined us a few moments later. "I was just gathering our things," he said, handing me Octo-Cat's bundled up leash. "And telling Breanne that I would be happy to apply a new coat of paint myself."

Right, to cover the huge damage I'd made with my light pencil marks.

"I hired you to make things easier for me. Not harder," Breanne said with a scowl.

"Sorry," I apologized for all of us. "It was one-hundred percent my fault."

Breanne regarded me coldly. "Oh, I know. That's why I want you off my brother's case."

A pit of fear formed deep in my stomach. This wasn't supposed to be happening. Charles and I were supposed to take our new theory about the killer's height and use it to clear Brock and save the day just in time. That would be much, much harder if Breanne stood in our way.

How could I explain this all without making her angrier? I didn't know, but I at least had to try. "But..."

"But nothing. All you're doing is making a mess of my sale property and distracting my lawyer from the job he's supposed to be doing."

"Brock's lawyer," I corrected without thinking.

Breanne fumed, stomping a heeled foot on the kitchen tile for added emphasis. "Yep. I definitely never want to see you again or your therapy animals. I'll also be having a talk with Mr. Thompson about my grave disappointment with his firm's performance to date."

I gulped and forced myself to keep quiet even though my instinct was to either defend myself or accuse her. Yo-Yo tensed in my arms and growled at Breanne.

"What is it with small scrappy dogs and their hatred for me?" Breanne asked flippantly as she shoved our entire party toward the door. "The homeowners had one just like this. It was the most irritating thing. Definitely reminded me why I'm a cat person."

"Did she say cat person?" Octo-Cat asked, quickening his pace so he could rub against the realtor's ankles. The whole thing was uncomfortably flirtatious, and I seriously had no idea what my tabby expected to gain from such an exchange. "I think I like this one," he purred.

Breanne bent down to pet his striped head, softening a bit as she stroked his silky fur.

"Oh, yeah! I like her very much!" Octo-Cat said, flipping onto his side and presenting his belly. What a traitor.

She sighed. "I guess I can hold off on the call to

Thompson, if only for this little cutie. But I still don't want you working on my case anymore."

"Noted," I answered coolly.

"What was that about?" I demanded once Charles, the animals, and I were tucked securely back in his car.

"What?" Octo-Cat shrugged, still calm and collected since the car hadn't begun to move yet. "Sometimes a guy just needs a little bit of attention from a pretty lady. Besides, I really saved your butt back there, so I wouldn't be complaining if I were you."

I groaned and shook my head. If I wasn't careful, I'd soon have a killer migraine.

"What did he say?" Charles asked, gesturing toward Octo-Cat with his chin.

"Never mind," I murmured.

Charles didn't push me any further on that, but he did ask, "Where to now? I think we need some time to catch up with the animals, and I doubt they'd be welcomed back at the firm."

"No," I agreed thoughtfully. "But I know somewhere even better we can go. Take a left out of here."

* * *

Nan answered the door in a rose-printed kimono so long it pooled at her feet. Her all-white hair clung to her jawline in a stylish bob that included a thick shelf of bangs that fell just above her brow.

"Looking good," I said, pushing straight into her house. This had been my home until about six months ago, when Nan had forced me to get a place of my own as part of the whole growing up thing. Even still, I visited her at least a couple times per week. She wasn't just the woman who'd raised me, but she was also my best friend and the person I trusted most in this entire world.

That's why I'd brought everyone here now.

Both animals followed me inside as I hooked a thumb back at Charles. "This is Charles. He's the head attorney on the case you helped me with the other day."

Wow, had it really only been two days since our dead-end trip to the printing company? *Unreal.*

"He's cute," Nan said, batting her eyelashes.

Charles cleared his throat and glanced toward the ground, which gave me the giggles. Nan had always been a shameless flirt, but she did it for fun, not to land a date. It had been more than ten years since Gramps passed on to a better place, and she hadn't taken on a boyfriend since. I doubted she'd make an exception for Charles, no matter how handsome we both found him. Besides, she'd no doubt soon associate him with the Hayes's double murder the way I did now.

Turning back toward me, Nan asked, "Here to work on the case?"

"Yup, you up for helping us out?" I led our party into the dining room as it had the best work area to seat all of us.

"Oh, dear, you know me," she answered, making eyes at Charles again. "I'm always up for anything."

He blushed, not quite knowing what to do with the geriatric flirt. "Actually, I'm not sure…"

"You can trust Nan," I insisted.

"I'll sign a Non-Disclosure Agreement," she added.

Charles looked trapped, but ultimately agreed with a shrug. "Fine," he said. "Do you have a printer I can use to print that NDA for you?"

Nan led him to the little office she kept upstairs, then returned to join me and the animals in the formal dining room. "Does he know about…?" She widened her eyes at Octo-Cat. "Well, you know."

"I'm afraid he does," I said with a groan. That was probably another reason why Charles and I could never become an item.

Nan sucked air through her teeth and shook her head in disappointment. "You shouldn't just go around blabbing your secret, dear. It's really not wise."

"Trust me, I didn't." I took a quick moment to catch her up on the whole blackmail scenario.

When Charles returned with his printed form, Nan hit him on the chest.

"Ouch," he mumbled. "What was that for?"

"You're lucky my granddaughter is such a forgiving person. If you ever blackmail her again, though, you'll have to answer to someone much less forgiving. Me." She pulled herself onto tiptoe and stared at him menacingly despite her small stature.

"Yes, ma'am," he answered at once as he clutched the NDA to his chest defensively. He almost looked afraid to offer it to Nan now.

I rolled my eyes at them both. "Enough posturing. We've got a lot of work to do and not much time to do it."

Charles unpacked his messenger bag and began

to lay out papers on the table, while Nan excused herself to make a pot of coffee. I took the opportunity to head to Nan's little office so that I could print out the photos I had taken while at the Hayes's house.

When I returned, Octo-Cat sat in the middle of the table, shedding all over everything as he flopped his tail back and forth.

"He wouldn't move," Charles told me with a frown.

"Keeping myself front and center is the best way to ensure you protect me from Dum-Dum," Octo-Cat explained. "I don't want you getting so caught up in your work that you forget all about the handsome cat who made this all possible."

Ugh, he was so vain. And even more stubborn.

"What did I tell you about calling him Dum-Dum?" I asked in irritation.

Octo-Cat yawned unapologetically. "Hey, I calls 'em like I sees 'em."

"Well, if you're not going to cooperate with us, then we're not going to cooperate with you. Oh, Yo-Yo!" I called, grabbing the cat and placing him on the floor so that the dog could slobber him with kisses.

Octo-Cat screeched, got puffy-tailed, and fled in

the direction of the kitchen, shouting kitty curses the whole way.

Nan appeared a couple minutes later, holding the tabby in her arms and stroking him kindly. "What did you do to this poor guy?" she demanded.

"Don't believe a word he says," I shot back. "He is not the victim he makes himself out to be."

"Oh, hush. He's just an innocent little kitty," Nan argued, peppering the smug feline with kisses. Even though she couldn't talk to animals the way I can, sometimes it felt like it. This was one of those times.

Charles couldn't help but chuckle. "How does it feel when the tables are turned on you, *hmmm?*"

Octo-Cat laughed, too, but not kindly. "Your nan likes me better than you," he teased, then actually had the audacity to stick his tongue out at me to add an extra layer of awfulness.

Nan put him down on the table, then returned to the kitchen to fetch the coffee.

"See?" Octo-Cat said. "If you won't appreciate me, I can always find someone else who does."

I picked him up again and was ready to give him back to Yo-Yo when Nan returned and scolded me. "You leave that handsome boy alone. He's such a good cat. Isn't he?"

Octo-Cat laughed again and immediately moved to Nan's side of the table where he snuggled up against her chest and purred at a ridiculous volume.

"By the way, here's your form," she said, pushing the Non-Disclosure Agreement in Charles's direction. "Now catch me up on the case."

I took a deep breath and explained everything.

"Huh," Nan said, sitting back in her chair pensively. "You sure have a doozy on your hands, but I think I have an idea."

I couldn't wait to hear what she had to say.

14

All eyes zoomed to Nan, even Yo-Yo's despite the fact he still didn't know what we were investigating, and I was pretty sure he couldn't understand any of us humans, either.

"Well, here's what I think..." my eccentric grandmother said, placing the Yorkie in her lap, much to Octo-Cat's annoyance.

He skittered across the table and back to my side. "Yuck. Dog germs," he said with an exaggerated twitch.

"I think," Nan continued in a baby voice directed at Yo-Yo. "That nobody's tried buttering this little guy up. You keep putting him in all these excitable situations and expecting him to be able to perform. Why not spend a little time getting to know him, making him feel comfortable, and then broaching the...?"

She hesitated before deciding on the word she needed to finish her sentence. "Um, conversation," Nan concluded with an awkward smile.

Charles and I looked to each other and shrugged.

"I guess it's worth a try," I said with a quick nod. I'd hoped she would stay with me and Charles to study the photos and files some more, but once Nan had an idea, it was hard to get her to focus on anything else. Actually, she was kind of like Yo-Yo in that way.

"Great." Nan stood, still clutching the terrier to her chest delicately. "You two get back to your work with those grisly photos, and I'll work on plying the key witness."

"We don't actually know that he saw anything. It's possible that—" Charles corrected, but stopped short when I placed a hand on his wrist and shook my head.

"Just let her do her thing, and we'll do ours," I said. "Now help me pull out the testimonies of all the women involved in the case—officers, witnesses, friends, neighbors, coworkers, anyone we have."

We shuffled through the papers, having all but memorized the order of the statements and evidence. It didn't even take five minutes to pull out the documents we needed.

"Now," I said, appraising our work. "Are there any men that we know for sure are my height or shorter?"

Charles thought for a few moments before handing me a couple of additional files. "This one is a colleague of Bill's from Bayside Printing Company, and that's one of the potential buyers from the open house."

I fanned everything out before us, attempting to group similar people together. We had one group for colleagues, one for people from the open house, one for friends and family, and one for miscellaneous folks who had somehow been called into the case, such as police officers or crime scene cleaners. Most documents weren't official testimonies at all, but rather bio sheets Charles had made himself before I joined the case.

"Let's go through them all one at a time,"

Charles suggested, reaching for the colleagues stack. We spent the next hour talking through each person and taking notes about who had either means, motive, or opportunity. For those that had more than one of those, we added a star to their sheet and placed them in a new pile.

After all that work, we were left staring at our two most probable suspects: the daughter and the realtor, Michelle Hayes and Breanne Calhoun.

I sighed and leaned back against my chair. "I keep hoping the facts will line up differently, but it really looks like one of these two is to blame."

Charles crossed his arms and shook his head, staring me directly in the eye as he defended our —or at least my—prime suspect. "No way. I know Breanne can be a bit brusque, but she didn't do it."

"Maybe so," I said, even though I still hadn't even come close to clearing the rude realtor in my mind. I like to think I learned my lesson from investigating Ethel Fulton's death. I'd been so convinced of who the killer was that I wouldn't even consider anyone else—and ended up putting myself in a very dangerous position besides.

Still, from everything I'd seen and heard so far, Breanne made sense. Maybe if I eased Charles into this realization a little more slowly, he'd put his hesitation aside and finally see things my way.

"Okay, so then let's discuss the daughter. How do you explain the fact that Michelle has more or less disappeared into thin air?"

"She hasn't disappeared," Charles argued this point, too. If we kept disagreeing over every single possibility, we might as well hand over Brock's conviction now.

"She's just not answering our calls," he said, tapping his pen on the table and frazzling my nerves.

"Okay, then where is she?" I demanded, grabbing the pen and moving it out of his reach.

Charles sighed and folded his hands in front of him. "At her college up state."

"Well, given that we have no other leads to pursue, I think I know where we're headed next."

"It will be a waste of time," he insisted with another heady sigh.

"Charles," I said gently. "Please. We have nothing else at this point. We at least have to try. For Brock."

"Fine. For Brock," he answered in defeat.

"Good," I said, even though his lack of enthusiasm made it an empty victory. "Let me go check with Nan and Yo-Yo. C'mon, Octo-Cat." I roused my tabby from his nap and motioned for him to follow me.

"Are we finally getting somewhere with all of this?" my cat asked after letting out a massive yawn.

"Soon, I hope," I said diplomatically.

Charles groaned and laid his forehead on the table as we walked away.

"Oh, hi, dears!" Nan cried as Octo-Cat and I joined her in the living room. "Yo-Yo and I are having a great time getting to know each other out here. Aren't we, boy?"

The terrier barked, and Nan praised him profusely.

"Well, she's lost at least ten points in my book," Octo-Cat said drolly. "It's always a shame when a good human falls to the dog side. I must say, I never expected this kind of betrayal from Nan. You, maybe, but definitely not her."

"She's not changing allegiances," I said as he jumped to the back of the couch and settled in. "She's just doing what she can to help out."

"Says you," he complained, shaking his head in disgust.

"Is everything okay?" Nan asked with a quick glance toward the perturbed kitty.

"It's fine, or at least it will be. Hey, Octo-Cat," I called to get his attention again.

"What?" he whined, mid-paw lick.

"You can take a bath later," I scolded. "The whole point of us coming out here was to see if Yo-Yo has anything new to say. Could you please ask him if he remembers anything new?"

"No, not like that," Nan interjected, continuing to pet the Yorkie enthusiastically. "Tell him his new friend Nan would like to know if anyone has hurt his family that he can remember and if he can tell us about it."

"Barf," Octo-Cat responded before shouting, "Hey, Dum-Dum!"

The terrier's head immediately snapped toward him. It definitely didn't help that Yo-Yo had started responding to the cat's cruel nickname for him.

Octo-Cat asked his question exactly as Nan had worded it, which caused the other animal to whimper and bury his face in Nan's lap. The fact that he wasn't yipping in terror was definitely progress.

My bored-looking cat nodded as he listened to the little dog, who had now lifted his head to look directly at Octo-Cat as he made sad puppy noises.

When Yo-Yo grew quiet again, Octo-Cat said, "Wow. I'm actually really surprised that worked."

I sat up straighter in my excitement. "What did he say?"

"He said it was really dark that night and he couldn't see well, but the person who hurt his mom and dad had red hair. He also wants to know when he can go back to his family."

The poor dog still didn't know he wouldn't be seeing his parents again, but he had finally given us enough to finish clicking all the pieces together. Red hair could only mean...

"So it was Breanne!" I shouted triumphantly. "I knew it!"

"Good kitty," I called back to Octo-Cat as I marched back to Charles in the dining room.

"Do not call me kitty," Octo-Cat growled after me, but from the note of happiness in his voice, I could tell the correction was just to remain consistent in his attempts to train me out of certain behaviors he didn't much appreciate.

"Did you hear?" I said, placing a palm on each side of the table and leaning toward Charles, who still looked utterly defeated.

"You think it was Breanne," he answered. When

he lifted his head, one of our case documents was stuck to his cheek. "Why?"

"Yo-Yo doesn't know they're dead, but he remembers them getting hurt. He said it was late at night, which matches up with what we know about the crime."

Charles finally looked as excited as I felt. "And?"

"He said it was dark so he couldn't see well, but that the person who hurt them had red hair. That could only be Breanne."

"Think again," Charles said, pulling out his phone and browsing through his email. When he handed it back to me, there was a young woman with bright red locks who looked vaguely familiar even though I wasn't sure I'd ever seen her before.

"Who's that?" I demanded.

"That's Michelle Hayes."

Uh oh.

We stared at each other for a moment before I finally came up with an argument. "But wouldn't Yo-Yo recognize his own sister?" I sputtered.

Charles frowned. "Not necessarily. Especially if it was too dark to make things out clearly."

"So what now?" I asked, gnawing on one of my few untouched fingernails as nerves overtook me.

"Road trip!" Nan cried from the other room.

Charles nodded. "It's our last shot at solving this in time to stop your mother's story."

Shoot, he was right. Even though just minutes earlier I'd been the one insisting we pay Michelle a visit, I felt much more anxious knowing that she may actually be the killer.

15

FRIDAY

The next morning, I woke up before Octo-Cat for what was probably one of the first times ever in our strange relationship. The alarm on my phone sounded at five thirty and I had to nudge him awake so that we could both get ready for the long day ahead.

In hindsight, I really wished we had gone to bed earlier the night before, but when Mom joined us at Nan's, we all wanted to hear her opinion on the progress we'd made so far.

"I have to admit," she told us, shaking her head. "It really seems like you're right about Brock not having done it."

Mom offered to hold the story longer, but I

insisted that she wouldn't have to. We would solve this thing before the six o'clock news was set to air, and we'd give her the exclusive true story, too.

Charles didn't share my optimism, but he did agree to wake up before dawn so we could make the long drive to Michelle's college where we'd grill her live and in person so we could finally uncover the important answers we'd been missing all this time.

Predictably, Yo-Yo was excited for our big road trip, even though we hadn't told him we were going to see his human sister.

I'd offered Octo-Cat the opportunity to stay at home, but he refused to get left out of the action. This worried me, because he had made zero progress in dealing with his car phobia and we had a very long drive ahead of us that day. Because I knew it would be impossible to change his mind, I decided to help him out. With his permission, I slipped some crushed-up medicine into his morning meal. It was just the kitty Benadryl his vet had previously prescribed in case of emergency, but it did cause him to snooze for a large part of our journey—and for that, everyone was very thankful indeed.

He really did look like an angel when he wasn't

insulting me, or clawing me, or questioning my life choices in general. And I suspected he was also starting to enjoy our crime-solving gig, even though for the time being it included a dog.

Nan joined us for the road trip, too. Yes, now that she'd been brought up to speed, she insisted on coming along for the ride. "In case Yo-Yo needs a friend," she'd said, making me wonder why I was the one who'd gained the ability to talk to animals when it seemed she was the one who understood them so much better.

Despite trying hard not to, I snoozed for part of the trip right along with Octo-Cat. After all, I didn't have Bethany to make coffee for me, and I'd already thrown out my home coffee maker for fear of sustaining another near-death experience, or worse —gaining weird, new superpowers. Luckily, Nan was more than happy to keep Charles company while Octo-Cat and I caught up on our beauty sleep.

"Rise and shine!" Nan shouted from behind me, forcing me to wake up again. Yes, indeed, the previously absent sun was now shining bright and high in the sky.

"We're here," Charles announced, maneuvering

his car into the guest parking lot that serviced our suspect's small liberal arts college.

"So what's the game plan?" Nan asked eagerly, leaning forward with a hand on the edge of each of our seats.

"Didn't you figure out the plan on the way over?" I asked in irritation. If I'd have known they were just going to shoot the breeze, I never would have allowed myself to nod off when there was still work to be done.

"Route One is lovely this time of year," Nan answered in a cheery tone. "We were too busy admiring the scenery to worry about what we'd do when we got here. Besides, you seem to be the designated worrier of the bunch. So, why don't you make the plan?"

I slapped a palm against my forehead. "I guess that's what I get for sleeping on the job."

Octo-Cat woke up and yawned in my face, sending a giant whiff of tuna breath straight up my nostrils. Let me tell you, it worked better than a double shot of espresso to snap me wide awake.

"It's a small college, so I guess let's just ask around," I said with a sigh, hating that this was now our plan. Then I realized we had one very distinct advantage we hadn't considered yet. "Maybe it's time to let Yo-Yo in on who we're here to see. He may even be able to sniff her out for us."

Before Charles had a chance to either agree or disagree, Octo-Cat relayed the message to the Yorkie, who responded immediately and with great enthusiasm to the idea.

"He's ready," Octo-Cat said as he stretched his legs and spine to finish waking up himself. Miraculously, he only hissed at me once while I worked the harness onto him.

Nan had a much harder time readying Yo-Yo, who continuously threw himself against the car door in his eagerness to reunite with Michelle.

Once both animals were safely leashed, we were on our way. As we walked around the seaside campus, it struck me that we were probably one of the strangest groups of five who'd ever wandered these paths. It was still only about nine in the morning, which meant the campus was mostly empty, but that didn't stop the people we did come across from sending pointed stares our way.

I smiled at each as they passed, but by the time the third or fourth person grimaced our way without so much as a proper "good morning," I'd had enough.

"So what if I'm walking my cat on a leash?" I

called, holding my chin high. They couldn't possibly judge me any harsher than I already judged myself. "He likes to get some fresh air, too. And why should dogs have all the fun?"

"Yes!" Octo-Cat cheered, skipping a little as he ran beside me. "Now you get it. You finally get it!"

Yo-Yo stopped abruptly and went rigid, making the same pointing gesture he'd taken on when first seeing the sign for Calhoun Realty. This time his gaze was fixed on a three-story stone building that lay across a neat and tidy lawn.

He woofed once, twice, then stopped.

"He says his sister is in that building," Octo-Cat translated.

"Is that a dorm?" I asked my human companions.

Charles jogged around the front and read the sign. "Yes, it is," he said when he returned, not even the least bit winded from the tiny burst of exercise.

"He wants to see his sister," Octo-Cat said as the Yorkie began to whimper and pad his paws on the ground impatiently.

"I'm going in," Nan said, forging confidently ahead.

"Wait. Why you?" Charles demanded.

"None of us are relatives, but I'd wager whatever security they have in this place is far less likely to question a kindly old lady." Nan paused for a moment. When neither of us argued with her, she straightened her posture and asked, "The mark's name is Michelle Hayes, right?"

The mark? What? Had Nan been watching those con man adventure movies again? She was really getting way to in to this.

Now that I was awake enough to notice things a bit better, I realized that she had actually put together an elderly granny costume, complete with a knitted shawl and a high-waisted skirt. The ensemble was so very not her that it could only be intentional. She'd had this plan all along but hadn't told me because she'd known I'd argue about her forging ahead alone.

Well, she was right about that much.

"I'm coming with you," I said, handing Octo-Cat's leash to Charles before trailing after her.

Charles grabbed me by my shoulder, forcing me to stop short. "She's right. We'll wait here until you come back or text us."

Nan nodded.

Charles nodded.

I groaned and motioned for Nan to carry on her

way. "Are they even going to let Yo-Yo into the dorms?" I called after her.

"Only one way to find out," Charles answered as we both watched Nan turn the corner to the front of the building.

"I don't like this," I pouted. "And I don't think Michelle did it."

"Yes, we've established what you think," my companion said with a groan.

"It's not just that I think Breanne's hiding something," I explained. "I mean, why would Michelle kill her own parents? And wouldn't Yo-Yo have recognized his own sister?"

"I don't know," Charles answered coolly. "But you're the one who insisted we come out here. Remember?"

"Only so we can eliminate Michelle and see if she has any direct proof that points to Breanne," I reminded him. Yes, I'd vowed not to jump to conclusions after my wrong assumptions nearly got me killed on the last case, but this was different. Yo-Yo had more or less identified Breanne already, and she was still the only person in the whole world he seemed to dislike. That had to be more than a simple coincidence.

Charles seemed far less convinced. "Well, I guess we'll see," he said with a shrug.

"Yeah, I guess we will."

Neither of us said anything more as we waited for Nan to return, although I sent out a quiet prayer that she'd have a ready and willing partner to help us finish our investigation once and for all.

Time was ticking away fast.

16

Nan reappeared about fifteen minutes later. At her side stood a fiery-haired, freckle-faced girl wearing pajama pants that had been liberally patterned with smiling cartoon tacos.

"Hello, darlings," Nan sang out proudly. "This is Mitch Hayes."

"Yeah. Nobody's called me Michelle since grade school," the college student explained before plopping a kiss right on Yo-Yo's fuzzy head. The little dog looked as if he were floating on a cloud as Mitch hugged and doted on him.

"Thanks for coming out to talk to us," Charles said. He rose and offered his hand to Mitch, and she struggled to adjust the terrier in her arms to accept

his greeting, leading to a rather awkward introduction.

"Why weren't you answering any calls?" I
demanded. Maybe I was being a tad rude, but none
of us had time to waste if we wanted to meet my
mother's deadline for clearing Brock.

The girl shrugged. "I dropped my phone in a
toilet a couple weeks ago and haven't felt the need
to replace it since I'm pretty much always on my
computer or tablet, anyway."

"But why not return any of the many, many
calls from people trying to get in touch with you?"
Charles asked, crooking his eyebrow.

"I was sick of people calling to make themselves
feel better about offering condolences while only
making me feel worse with the constant reminders
that my parents are dead." She buried her face in
the Yorkie's fur and mumbled, "Maybe I don't want
to talk about the fact my parents were murdered in
cold blood."

Nan placed an arm around Mitch and pulled
her in close. "You two can stop with the third
degree now. Mitch doesn't have to help us, but she's
kindly agreed to anyhow."

"Thank you, Mitch," I said, offering a smile I

hoped would get through to her. "We do really appreciate it."

She kicked at the ground and kept her eyes focused there. "So you really think this Brock guy is innocent?"

I placed a gentle hand on her shoulder and waited for her to look up at me. "We know he is."

She shivered beneath my hand and her face took on a new pallor. "That means the person who killed my parents is still out there."

I let go of her shoulder and grabbed my shoulder instead. "Yeah."

"Tell me what you need me to do." Mitch set her mouth in a determined line, her brows furrowed in anger.

"Over here." Charles cleared his throat and motioned for everyone to sit on a nearby retaining wall. "We need you to tell us anything that could help us identify the real killer."

Poor Mitch looked a bit lost. "But you have my statement, right? I already told the cops everything I could think of."

"We do, but do you mind if we ask you a few more questions in light of recent things we've learned?" Charles asked, reaching into his bag. I seriously hoped he didn't plan to pull out the crime scene photos right now. Mitch shouldn't have to see that.

Even before Charles could find what he was searching for, a sudden burst of tears fell from the girl's bright blue eyes.

"Oh for goodness's sake, you two. Slow down a bit. Can't you see this is hard on her?" Nan grumbled, pressing the girl's head into her shoulder. "You just go ahead and cry all the tears you need to cry. That's right. Nan is here for you now."

Yo-Yo whined and licked his sister's face, offering a hesitant tail wag.

As I watched them and tried to come up with a new way to approach questioning Mitch, Octo-Cat pawed at my shoulder.

"Excuse me," he said, shocking me with his sudden politeness. "Dum-Du—I mean, *the dog* says he remembers who hurt his owners now. Also, he says he thinks his humans might even be dead."

"He remembers?" I asked, not even caring when Mitch lifted her head to study us curiously. "I thought he said it was too dark to see."

"Yes, but he smelled everything just fine, and apparently remembers who it was now," Octo-Cat explained slowly.

Yo-Yo fixed his eyes on me and gave an urgent bark.

"So, yeah." Octo-Cat dropped his voice to a hissy whisper and leaned in close. "Can I finally just tell him already?"

"Tell him what? Oh…" That his owners are dead. Yo-Yo still didn't know for sure. I nodded my agreement. "Yeah, I think it's time."

Octo-Cat spoke to Yo-Yo calmly and much kinder than he ever had before. When he'd said all he needed to say, I waited for the inevitable high-pitched screeching and crazy escape attempts from Yo-Yo, but he just let out a soft whimper and snuggled in closer to Mitch.

"Why isn't he freaking out?" I asked my cat.

Octo-Cat had something akin to respect written across his face. I couldn't be one-hundred percent sure, since I'd never seen him make that expression before and it didn't seem likely I'd ever see it again, either.

"He wants to be strong for his human," he told me.

I brought a hand to my chest and said, "Awww, that's so sweet."

Octo-Cat shrugged his little kitty shoulders.

"Yeah, dogs might not be the smartest, but they are loyal. I guess that's their one redeeming quality."

Yo-Yo licked Mitch a few more times, then untangled himself from her arms and came to sit right next to me. He let out a string of four or five barks, keeping his eyes trained on me the whole time he spoke.

"He didn't see much, but he remembers her smell now," Octo-Cat said. He lifted a paw to his mouth, but then thought better of beginning a new grooming session at this key investigative moment and dropped his paw back to the ground.

"Her, right." So far everything was lining up with what Charles and I already knew—or at least theorized—and things weren't looking very good for our realtor friend. "Who was it?"

Sure enough, Octo-Cat confirmed my suspicions with what he said next. "He says it was the lady selling the house."

"Breanne, I knew it!" I shouted before turning to Charles. "Give me that picture of Breanne from her flyer, please."

He stared at me wordlessly for a moment before finally reaching into his messenger bag and retrieving the requested photo.

"Is this her?" I asked, holding the paper up to Yo-Yo.

He let out a bark that quickly turned into a growl.

"See!" I said, shoving the paper back at Charles. "You let your crush on Breanne blind you to the truth. It was her this whole time."

Octo-Cat pawed me again. This time with a bit of claw.

"Ouch!" I cried. "What now?"

"That's not what he said," he told me with a smug smirk.

Not Breanne? How could that possibly be? We already knew it wasn't Mitch. Glendale wasn't very big. How many five foot seven redheaded killers could we possibly have in our small town?

I widened my eyes at him, waiting.

"He said it wasn't the lady on the paper," Octo-Cat explained, visibly losing patience with each word. "It was the other one."

"What?" I asked as my heart crashed to my feet. "All this just to find out it really was Brock all along?"

Octo-Cat turned to the terrier, and the two spoke quietly back and forth for a couple minutes before he looked back to me.

"Not the man," he said. "The other lady."

"Charles," I said, reaching out my hand. "Give me a photo of Brock to show Yo-Yo."

Mitch, who'd kept quiet during this whole exchange until now, piped up. Her eyes were wide and unblinking as she asked, "Are you actually talking with that cat?"

"It gets less weird the more you're around it," Nan explained with a kind chuckle.

"Looks like the cat's out of the bag," Charles added with a laugh that was way too generous for his bad joke.

I didn't have the time to worry about some college student learning my secret. I was so close to figuring this out, and just in the nick of time, too. We only had about ten hours before my mom's story would run. Maybe—just maybe—it would actually be enough.

Charles held up the picture of Brock, and Yo-Yo made a high-pitched yipping noise.

"Not him," Octo-Cat translated.

"Then who does he mean when he says it's the other one?" I complained. Something just wasn't clicking. Maybe Yo-Yo wasn't the key to solving the case, after all.

"Brock *is* the other one," I insisted, speaking to

Octo-Cat but keeping my gaze on Yo-Yo as I did so. "Who else is there?"

"I'm calling Breanne," Charles announced already mid-dial.

"Give me that," I said, yanking his cell phone right out of his hand.

"Hello?" Breanne answered full of an energy and friendliness I certainly hadn't heard from her before.

I caught the eye of each of my companions and raised a finger to my lips to let them know they needed to be quiet. "Hello, Breanne. It's me, Angie Russo, the paralegal on your brother's case."

"I thought I told you I didn't want you working on it anymore," she growled, every ounce of kindness having evaporated within a split second.

"I'm off the case after today," I explained quickly. "But Charles asked me to drive up to Michelle Hayes's school and see if I could find her. She only had a few minutes before her class started, but she told me the realtor did it."

Yeah, like I was about to confess my strange abilities to someone who already hated me.

"Impossible," Breanne spat back. "I didn't do it, and neither did my brother. It's awfully funny that she's blaming me now when she swore she didn't have a clue in her statement to the police."

I made a tight fist and then let it go, bracing myself for what came next. "If you didn't, then who did? I mean, who else could she possibly mean?"

Breanne made a series of infuriated noises that started with a huff and ended with a yell. "That's it! I'm definitely calling Mr. Thompson to file an official complaint."

"Please just answer the question," I insisted, praying she wouldn't hang up on me before offering anything good.

"The realtor," Breanne yelled. "That could mean absolutely anybody. Do you know there are more than three-thousand realtors licensed just in the state of Maine? It could have been any of the ones who showed up at the open house or had a showing before that, or even the one who was helping them to buy their new house. Anyone could have had access to the lockbox. Anyone could have killed them."

"Wait," I said. My breathing hitched, and I shook from the sudden excitement of my realization. "Go back."

"Anyone could have access. The fact you insist on blaming me when I'm the one paying—"

As much as I knew she liked yelling at me, I had to cut Breanne off in order to keep her focused. "Not that. Before," I begged.

"Despite your fondness for blaming me, Michelle could have literally been talking about any other realtor. If she had some insider information, then why hasn't she shared before now?"

"Forget about that for now," I said. "You mentioned another realtor. You're not the one helping buy their new house?"

Breanne drew in a sharp breath. Maybe she was finally beginning to understand now. "No. I mean, I wanted to, but they already had someone picked out before they came to me to list their house."

"Do you know who that other realtor was?" I asked, then held my breath as I waited.

Her answer would determine everything.

17

All eyes watched me as I waited for Breanne's answer to come through the line. Even my heart seemed to beat more quietly for fear of missing a single word.

"I don't understand why this is important," the realtor grumbled, disappointing us all.

Charles grabbed the phone from my hands and practically shouted into the speaker. "Breanne, it's Charles. We think the other realtor is the key to clearing your brother. Can you tell us who it is?"

I followed after Charles as he paced a small path, making sure I remained close enough to hear both sides of the conversation.

Surprisingly, Breanne seemed just as irritated with Charles as she had been with me. "Really?" she shot back sarcastically. "Because a couple seconds ago your assistant accused me of killing the Hayeses."

Charles shot daggers in my direction but kept his voice even for Breanne's benefit. "I promise that's not what she was doing. She just... has a hard time expressing herself clearly sometimes."

"I want her off my case," Breanne reminded him with a heavy sigh. "And you should really consider getting yourself a new assistant, anyway."

Charles's voice became small. "Could you please just—"

"Oh for Pete's sake!" Nan shouted, yanking the phone away from Charles and delivering it to Mitch, who stared down at it in confusion.

"Go ahead, honey," Nan coaxed. "Tell her who you are and what you want."

"Hi, this is Michelle Hayes," the girl sputtered into the phone.

Everyone grew silent again as we watched to find out what would happen next.

"Would you please tell me the name of the realtor helping my parents buy their new house?" Mitch asked, her voice shaky. I couldn't tell whether the fresh tears in her voice were authentic or for added dramatic effect, but I hoped they would work on the coarse woman on the other end of the line.

Of course, the phone had gotten too far away for me to clearly hear Breanne's response, but Mitch nodded along as the realtor said whatever she needed to say.

"Please," the girl said next, her voice cracking on that solitary word. "I just want to find out who killed my parents and make sure they're punished for it. Can you help?"

She listened some more, nodded a bunch, then turned to the rest of us and flashed a thumbs up sign before saying, "Great. Thank you so much for your help... Yes, we'll definitely do that... Bye."

"Well?" Nan practically shouted, ready to explode with excitement.

Mitch looked quite pleased with herself as she handed Charles's phone back to him. "She says she doesn't know off hand, but the info will be in the realtor database. She's looking it up now and will text the info to Charles. She said, um, that she prefers not to deal with the assistant anymore."

Of course. I was beginning to think Breanne's problem with me was much bigger than just me drawing on some walls, but honestly, it didn't really matter. Not when we still had a double murder to solve.

Charles shot me a sympathetic look. At that same moment, a new text notification flashed across the screen. "Sandra Lynn of Lighthouse Realty & Brokerage. Anyone recognize that name?" he asked, glancing toward each of us in turn.

We all shook our heads and waited as Charles returned his attention to the phone.

"Hold on," he said, squinting down at the phone. The clouds had just cleared, sending a direct beam of brightness down onto the campus. It was almost as if God Himself wanted to spotlight the importance of this moment.

"Breanne just sent a link," Charles explained as his fingers swept across the phone.

I slid close to him and stared at his slowly loading web browser. When the site finally did load, I recognized the woman splashed across its front page almost immediately. There she stood in front of a spiraled black and white lighthouse with her wavy red hair blowing softly in the breeze as she smiled and held up a giant, hulking *SOLD* sign.

"Is that the woman we ran into at the Little Dog Diner?" Charles asked. "The one who wanted our table?"

I blinked hard and looked again. Yes, that was her, too. The diner wasn't the place I first remembered seeing her, though. "She was at the Printing Company when Nan and I went to investigate. She said she was hoping to pick up an order before they closed for the evening. She was the reason I couldn't do any snooping around the storefront."

Understanding lit in Charles's eyes. "So that means she would have known at least Bill already, if not Ruth, too," he surmised.

I'd only ever rented, but something about that didn't make sense to me. "But if they were close enough to have her buy their new house, why wouldn't they have hired her to sell their existing one, too?"

Charles shrugged. "People don't always use the same realtor for both transactions, but I do find it weird she wasn't brought into the investigation before."

"It says here she's based out of Misty Harbor, which would explain why we saw her at the diner," I pointed out. "That's in Misty Harbor, too."

Charles worried his lip, then asked, "Should we call her?"

"And let her know we're coming? Heck no!" Nan broke in, then once again stole the phone from

Charles. "Give me that," she said with a huff, then marched right up to Yo-Yo and held the device in front of his face.

The dog immediately growled and snapped at the air.

Nan had to jump back to avoid getting bitten.

Octo-Cat trotted over to my side. "He says—"

"Yeah, I don't think we need that one translated," I said with a giant smile. We'd done it. We'd really done it. And just in time, too.

"Let's go get our perp," Nan said, already marching back toward the parking lot. She paused a moment to call over her shoulder, "You coming, Mitch?"

The girl hopped off the half wall. "Let's do this!"

And just like that, we were all running back to the car—Charles, me, Nan, Mitch, Octo-Cat, and Yo-Yo—which we reached in record time for such a motley crew.

"It all lines up," I said between heavy breaths while my fingers fumbled with the seatbelt's clasp. "Sandra looks enough like Breanne that it confused Yo-Yo. They're also both realtors who were working with the Hayeses, which would have only added to his confusion."

"Plus, all humans look the same," Octo-Cat pointed out.

"And that," I said with a freeing laugh. Oh my gosh, we had done it. "Now we just have to prove it in a way that will hold up in court, and Brock will be a free man."

"You leave that to me," Nan said, cracking her knuckles on each hand as if readying for war.

"No way!" Charles answered for me. "You've already done more than enough."

"Hold on," I said calmly, doing my best to be the voice of reason. "We have a long drive ahead of us. Maybe we can reconsider all the facts we already know about the case in light of this new information and try to figure out what possible motive Sandra Lynn could have had for..." I stopped, remembering Mitch with was us now. "Well, you know."

"Sure," Charles answered, sending a sly grin in my direction. "Just so long as everyone stays awake this time."

"Hardy har har," I shot back. "This isn't a time for making jokes. It's a time for finding answers."

"Let's get you caught up, Mitch," Nan mumbled from the backseat, then placed a hand on the side of Charles's seat and mine. "Where's that briefcase of yours?"

"I have it here," I said, reaching down to grab it from my footwell. "Give me a minute to do some... um, tidying up, and then it's all yours." I grabbed each of the photos and the written reports describing the crime scene and stashed them in the glove box, then handed Charles's bag back to Nan.

Nan began to explain what we already knew to her rapt audience of one.

"So are we done now?" Octo-Cat asked from the cushion on my lap. "Case closed?"

"We're almost there," I assured him with a gentle pat on his head.

"How do we go from almost to all the way?" he asked with a growl. I tried not to take it personally since I knew how much he hated car rides, and I hadn't thought to bring him any Benadryl for our return trip home.

"I need to go home and sleep for the next six or seven days at least," he informed me with a weary sigh.

"Based on what Yo-Yo's told us, we have a very strong case against Sandra Lynn," I explained. "The only problem is that won't be enough for the other humans."

"Because he's a dog?" Octo-Cat asked.

I rolled my eyes. "I think you know why. Don't be such a smart aleck."

"So what now?" he insisted.

"Now we need to find evidence they'll accept without questioning our sanity in the process. So we already have the answer. Now we need to work backward to find the clues that support that answer. Make sense?"

"Yeah, but it sure seems like a lot of work." Octo-Cat's posture grew more rigid as Charles took a sharp turn. "You know you have another option. Right?"

"Oh, really, and what's that?" I challenged, placing a hand on his back to help steady him.

He flicked his tail with one giant movement before revealing, "Get a confession. *Duh.*"

Finally, all the TV he'd been watching lately seemed to have paid off. I was very glad he'd graduated from *Dora the Explorer* to *Law & Order,* which was no doubt what inspired this little nugget of wisdom.

Charles turned to study me briefly before training his eyes back on the road. "What did he say?"

Well, this created quite the conundrum. While I

didn't want to lie to Charles, I also knew he wouldn't be a big fan of the forced confession plan.

On my last case, I'd headed into trouble all my own and just barely managed to escape with my life. Well, this time I definitely wouldn't be making the same mistake.

Nope.

This time, I'd be sure to bring the cat with me when I marched straight into Sandra Lynn's office and demanded an explanation.

18

By the time we got back to Glendale, the noon sun already hung high in the sky. Nan invited everyone over to her house for lunch while they once again reviewed the evidence, this time trying to prove what Yo-Yo had revealed to us that morning.

I excused myself from the shindig by providing the very valid excuse of needing to take Octo-Cat home to use his litter box. They didn't need to know what I had planned after that quick pit stop.

"Okay, so what now?" Octo-Cat asked after visiting his little kitty box and wiping his paws off on the new mat I'd purchased expressly for his use.

"What do you mean?" I asked, searching the

fridge for some food I could quickly inhale to calm my growling stomach.

He regarded me with a piteous look. "What do you mean 'what do I mean?' *I mean* we're going to get that confession, right? I assumed we didn't talk about it in the car because you didn't want Upchuck to know the plan—not because you'd given up on it already."

While he made his harangue, I found an old but not yet expired package of string cheese shoved into the back of my vegetable drawer and grabbed a couple of pieces to tide me over. After tearing into the first with great aplomb, I peeled off a thick piece and shoved it in my mouth.

Then I attempted to answer my cat's concerns by saying, "Of course we're going to get the confession. I figured we could start with me pretending to be an interested client, and you hiding in your wicker bag."

Octo-Cat wrinkled his nose. "I hate that bag."

"Got any other ideas?" I challenged, putting another thick string of cheese into my mouth.

He paced back and forth on the table in frustration as he talked. "I do have ideas, but none that don't put at least one of my lives at risk. I'd be willing to make that sacrifice for the team, but something tells me you wouldn't."

"I only have one life, remember?" I probably should have been insulted that he kept forgetting— or at least completely disregarding—this very important fact, but right then I was too keyed up to care.

"Ahh, yes." Octo-Cat plopped his rear down and shook his head. "So fragile."

I inhaled the final stringy thing from my first cheese and opened the second package, rolling my eyes as I did. "Fine, I'm fragile, but I still think putting you in the bag for half an hour is preferable to the possibility of me dying. Don't you?"

Octo-Cat responded by lifting a rear leg over his head and licking his kitty bits.

"Um, excuse me? I'm talking to you!" Suddenly I had less of an appetite.

"What? I'm still thinking. Give me a minute here," he mumbled while he continued to groom himself. It was so nice to see that protecting my life held comparable importance to avoiding a perfectly normal smelling wicker bag. That whole superior sense of smell was a total excuse, and I knew it. The snobby cat claimed it stunk mostly because he hated that I'd picked it up at a charity thrift store.

"Fine," he said at last, dropping his leg back to the floor. "I'll get in the bag, but you owe me."

"I already owe you from the harness," I pointed out, regretting my big mouth instantly. I shoved another bite of string cheese in with the hope it would keep me from saying something else I'd come to regret.

What could only be described as an evil smile crept across his furry face. "Yes," he answered with a malicious laugh. "And the size of that favor just grew. Keep going, sweetheart. Daddy needs a new... well, everything."

Uck. I didn't know whether to be more afraid of the threat or disgusted by the manner in which he'd made it. I gulped down my anxiety and with it the too-large piece of unchewed cheese. It only took a millisecond to realize I was choking on the stupid thing.

Octo-Cat sat by and watched as I gestured wildly to my throat. He didn't so much as move a paw as I coughed and pounded on my chest, finally dislodging the misplaced morsel.

"What would you have done if I died?" I demanded, my voice hoarse. "I was choking, and you didn't even try to help!"

He yawned. "Oh, is that what that display was

all about? I thought you were just stalling for time. You know, if we don't hurry, Upchuck and the gang will come looking for us. Is that what you want?"

Ugh. I hated that he was right even more than I hated the complete lack of sympathy.

"Fine, let's go," I said after filling up my water bottle at the sink.

Octo-Cat followed me hesitantly. "No harness this time?"

"Nope," I said, grabbing my prize from the coat closet and holding it up for him to see. I looked forward to knowing he would suffer just a little bit. Such was the nature of our relationship. "Bag instead."

He raised his paw in a gesture I hadn't seen from him before. He must have learned that from one of his many kids' TV shows. "Um, I have a question."

I raised my eyebrows and motioned for him to go ahead.

"What is my role in all of this?"

"If anything bad happens, use your iPad to call for help. And if anything really bad happens, use your claws and attack. Can you do that for me?"

He nodded. "As long as you remember to bring my iPad."

I groaned and tracked back to the bedroom to retrieve his favorite toy. "Good?" I asked, tucking it into the rear pocket of the bag. This was such an odd way to prepare for what could be a risky situation, but it was a fair representation of what my life looked like now.

"One more thing," I told him as we made our way to the car. "I'm calling my mom."

"Why? Aren't I enough for you?"

"Trust me," I said with a laugh. "You're more than enough most days, but I did promise my mom a scoop. And I'm going to make sure we get it."

He still appeared confused. "Won't she try to stop you? Isn't that why you didn't let Charles or Nan know?"

"Yes, that's why I didn't tell them, but Mom doesn't worry the same way they do. She understands the need to do whatever it takes to get the story."

Octo-Cat climbed onto my lap and dug his claws into my thigh as I started the engine. "It's your life," he said.

What a great attitude for a wingman. If the time really did come to save my life, I hoped he would take the necessary actions. I felt less sure, though, after the brief choking incident.

I couldn't focus on that right now. I needed to save an innocent man from spending the rest of his life in prison. Last time I'd gotten caught because I hadn't realized I was walking into a dangerous situation. This time I knew and was prepared, too.

After buckling my seatbelt, I connected Octo-Cat's iPad to the car's Bluetooth and placed a voice-only FaceTime call to my mom.

She answered so fast, I didn't even hear it ring. "Hey, Angie. Any luck today?"

"As a matter of fact," I announced, speaking loudly to make sure she could hear me over the sound of the car's engine. "I'm on my way to Misty Harbor now. Think you can join me with a film crew?"

"It may take a little bit to get everyone together. We're not used to breaking news in Glendale. But I will be there as fast as I can. Any particular place?"

"Lighthouse Realty & Brokerage," I told her, rattling off the address.

"I'm impressed. How'd you find out who really did it?" she asked.

My daughterly heart swelled with pride, but still, I hesitated. She didn't know the truth about my abilities yet, and this didn't seem like the right time or the right method by which to tell her.

"It's a long story. Let's get it on camera," I said, knowing full well I would never, ever reveal my quirky powers on the local news. It would be hard enough just to tell Mom, but I knew that I'd be doing just that before the day was through.

"There's my smart daughter. That associate degree in communications really paid off. I still think you should go back for journalism. We'd make a great team, you and me."

"I'll think about it, Mom," I said, knowing full well the newsroom held zero appeal to me. I'd hate to be in direct competition with my ambitious mom, and I'd hate even more to have to work at her side every day. We definitely loved each other, but mostly in small doses.

She chuckled good-naturedly. "I know what that means, but you're right. Let's just focus on the story in front of us for now."

There was still one more thing I needed to say, and it was the hardest part. "Mom?"

"Yeah?"

"If you get a call from me within the next hour, even if—especially if—I'm not talking on the other end of the line, call the cops. Okay?"

She sucked in air through her teeth then asked, "Are you doing something dangerous?"

I sure hoped not.

"No. It's just a precaution," I lied. Of course, I knew that Sandra had killed before—*twice!*—and that there was no guarantee she wouldn't turn on me once she found out I'd uncovered and planned to expose her crimes.

"I guess it's always good to have a backup plan," Mom said resignedly. "I'll be up there soon."

"Okay," I responded. "Call me when you get there. My phone may be off, but I'll call back as soon as I can. And Mom?"

"Yeah?"

"I love you."

"Love you, too."

I took a deep breath and turned to Octo-Cat. "There," I said. "Now my mom's cell is the last number in your call history. Call her if there's any trouble, okay?"

His face looked grim. Whether he was finally beginning to see just how dangerous this situation could be for me or simply upset about the car ride, I couldn't say for sure.

The only thing I could say for sure was that we were going to catch a killer today. *No matter what.*

19

"It's go time," I muttered from the front seat of my car, which now sat parked in the small lot outside Lighthouse Realty & Brokerage. My hands shook as I grabbed my striped wicker bag from the passenger seat floor well and held it open for Octo-Cat to climb inside.

He growled but otherwise complied without too much complaint.

"Remember, your iPad is tucked into the back pocket," I informed him. "I'll keep your bag on my lap. If there's an emergency, jump out and knock the bag off my lap. That should make the iPad fall out onto the floor so you can use it."

"Understood," he said. "But what if it ends up upside down?"

"Let's pray it doesn't," I said, wishing I would have seen this flaw in my plan earlier. But we were here now, and I had to take action.

"Just put it in the bag next to me," he said, popping his head out of the bag to study me.

"But you don't like things touching you," I pointed out.

"It's an inconvenience, yes. But it would be much more inconvenient if you died and I had to train another human on my likes and dislikes."

"Aww, so you do love me, after all!" I cooed, slipping the iPad out of the back pocket and into the main compartment of the bag.

"Enough with the mushy stuff. Get in there and catch the bad guy," he said, lowering himself back into position.

Right. I took another deep breath and clambered out of the car, adjusting the bag carefully over my shoulder as I approached the front door. Hopefully Sandra would be in. I hadn't called ahead, preferring to play things by ear. Yes, I didn't have much of a plan, but hoped the acting genes in my family would come in handy.

When I pushed through the glass door, a little bell chimed to announce my arrival. The office smelled pleasant like warm vanilla, and the waiting area was flanked with two overstuffed couches and an inviting array of magazines. It even had a mini cooler filled with bottled water, several kinds of soda, and coffee shots.

Seeing that no one was waiting at the front desk, I took the opportunity to snag one of the cold coffee shots. Maybe I could buy these for myself at home. I popped the can open and took an appreciative swig, downing the entire thing in three big gulps.

Liquid courage?

I sure hoped so.

"Hello, and welcome to Lighthouse Realty & Brokerage," a woman's voice greeted me from across the room. "How can we help you?"

I glanced over and immediately recognized Sandra Lynn with her unmistakable curly red hair and that huge smile that I now knew hid dark secrets. I grabbed the straps on my bag, needing the connection to Octo-Cat to keep my wits about me and stay on task.

"Good afternoon," I said with what I hoped was a pleasant smile. "I'm here because I'd like to buy a house."

Sandra laughed, and the sound was startlingly shrill. I wonder if I would have been so put off by it without the knowledge of her after-hours criminal activity. "Well, I can certainly help with that. Why don't you come on back to my office?" She began taking sure, steady strides down the hall, and I followed after.

"You're in luck," she prattled on over her shoulder as we walked. "Usually walk-ins have to deal with one of our junior agents, but I just so happened to have a cancellation this afternoon. As the owner of this realty and the most experienced agent, I'll make sure you have the house of your dreams in no time at all."

She simpered at me as she stopped and waited for me to enter the small, dimly lit office ahead of her.

"That is lucky," I said with a polite smile of my own.

"What's your name, dear? And will this be your first time purchasing?" Sandra took a seat behind her desk and leaned forward slightly as we spoke.

"I'm Angela," I said, reaching forward to shake her hand. It wasn't quite a lie, but it wasn't quite the truth. Nobody called me Angela except Octo-Cat—and even then he only did it on occasion. "Yes, it's my first time," I finished.

"Well, let me give you a run-down of the basics," Sandra said, launching into a lengthy monologue that gave me time to search the office with my eyes. Nothing stood out as being particularly incriminating, but I hadn't exactly expected to find a bloody hammer sitting on top of her desk, either.

Sandra finished her speech and waited for me to say something, but I hadn't been paying close enough attention to figure out what.

"What are you looking for, dear?" she repeated. Her smile faltered somewhat as she waited for me to keep up my end of the exchange.

"Um..." I thought back to all the mental gymnastics Charles, Nan, Mitch, and I had done on the car ride home to Glendale. They all centered around the question: *What reason could a realtor possibly have to kill her clients?* Money seemed the safest bet. I didn't understand what all that entailed but decided to broach the subject delicately.

"I'd really like a nice three bedroom, but I'm worried I may not have enough money to make my dream house a reality."

She frowned briefly before shaking her head and bringing back the smile. "That's okay. We can work around it. What's your credit like?"

"It's pretty bad." Unfortunately, that part wasn't a lie.

She pressed her coral-colored lips together in a flat line. "Hmm."

"Is there anything you can do to help?" I asked, calling up my best impression of a desperate aspiring homeowner.

Sandra stiffened, taking a moment before answering. "There are government programs that may be able to help get you into a house. Your interest rate probably won't be that good, but that's the case for a lot of first-time buyers."

"Okay," I said helplessly.

"Why did you decide to buy now if money is so tight?" she asked.

I had to think fast to avoid suspicion, so I said the first thing that popped into my head. "Well, with my current rental, it feels like me and my cat are living on top of each other. We need some more space. Oh, and I have a dog, too. A Yorkie."

She blanched at this and swallowed before letting that shrill laugh loose again. "Sounds like you have your hands full," she said.

I'm not sure if I imagined it, but she definitely faltered upon the mention of "my" Yorkie. If I could push this topic a little further, maybe I could unsettle her enough to trick her into a confession.

"Are you a dog person?" I asked, hugging my

bag tight on my lap to reassure Octo-Cat, who no doubt hated not being able to join this particular conversation. After all, one of his favorite pastimes since meeting Yo-Yo was pointing out how superior cats are to dogs.

"I watched a dog for a friend once," Sandra answered, turning away from me to organize some papers. "I'm not sure I'm cut out for a dog companion myself, but since you are, let's get you a place with a fenced-in yard." She handed me a printed-out list triumphantly.

I puzzled over her words while pretending to review the listing. Watched a dog for a friend? Was she talking about Yo-Yo? Is that why he'd disappeared for a few weeks before turning back up at the Hayes's door where Charles then found him? And, if so, why hadn't Yo-Yo told us?

I thought his traumatic memory loss had been resolved once we reunited him with Mitch, but perhaps he'd still chosen to forget some of the other details that weren't directly pertinent to remembering who'd done it.

"I'm not sure this one is for me," I said, pushing the listing back across the desk. "Thank you, though."

"Have you done any shopping around online?

Those listings aren't always the most up to date, but if you have an idea of what you like, it could help me to refine our search."

She was very good at staying right on topic and pushing me closer to buying with each comment. It would take something major to knock her off her game. Luckily, I still had an ace up my sleeve.

"Actually..." I said, trying to still my shaking hands by hugging the wicker bag tighter to my chest. "There is a place I like out in Glendale. It's above my price range, but I'm hoping we might be able to get a good deal."

"I'm happy to negotiate with the homeowners to see what we can do," Sandra said with an ingratiating smile. "Is that the house you want? Are you ready to start putting together an offer?"

"Well, it is a really nice house. I guess we could try," I said, feigning hesitation.

She nodded enthusiastically. I'm sure it must be nice to make a big commission with hardly any work at all. She probably looked at me and saw a giant, sparkling dollar sign now. "Fabulous. Do you have the address?"

I pulled out my phone and pretended to search for information before rattling off the Hayes's address, which I already happened to know by heart.

Sandra didn't say anything in response—just sat there staring at me, so I added, "Like I said, I'm hoping we can get a good deal, because two people were murdered there."

"I don't think that's the house for you, dear," the realtor spat out at last.

"Why not?" I argued. "It's in a great location and has plenty of space for me and my pets. Can't we at least put in an offer and see?"

"I'd really urge you to consider a property with a less sordid history," she said, turning back to her files and pulling out another listing, seemingly at random. "This looks nice. How about this one?"

I didn't even look down at the paper. Keeping my eyes glued to hers, I licked my lips and said, "You said we could put in an offer, and that's what I want to do. Can we get started please?"

She shook her head. "I probably shouldn't be saying this, because it makes me look a little, well, like I'm not all there…" Sandra paused to laugh, but I kept my face neutral, waiting.

"But that place you mentioned?" she continued. "It's very, very haunted."

"Oh? Just a sec." I placed my bag on the floor

right in front of her oversized desk so that she wouldn't be able to see what I was doing unless she chose to stand up. I grabbed the iPad and motioned for Octo-Cat to creep out as well. Once both were settled on the floor and I confirmed that the tabby was indeed placing a call to my mom, I straightened back in my chair and returned my focus to an increasingly nervous-looking Sandra.

"It's haunted, huh?" I asked, shaking my head. "Well, how about that?"

She nodded eagerly; relief flashed across her face. "I know some people don't believe in ghosts and all, but they are there and very angry. It's best not to get involved with that mess."

"Wow. Hmm," I said, pretending to think this over carefully but only to buy us a little more time. If Octo-Cat could get Mom on the line before I showed my hand, she'd be able to hear what happened next. I heard a little murmur sound from the floor. That had to be her.

"What was that?" Sandra asked, shifting her gaze around the room to find the source of the speaker.

"Wait. I have a question," I blurted out to draw her attention back to me. "You say the ghosts are angry. Is that because you murdered them?"

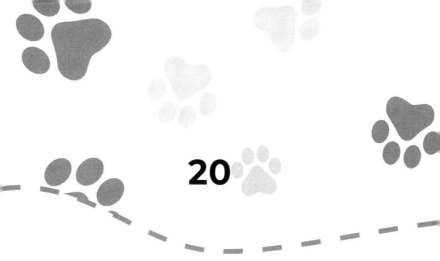

20

"Why, I've never been so insulted in all my life. Go! Get out of my office!" the realtor cried. All traces of her earlier smile completely wiped clean from her face, which now pinched in rage. Sandra popped to her feet so quickly, I instantly recoiled in fear.

And, in my attempt to stumble to a standing position, I stepped on Octo-Cat's tail.

He let out a terrible yowl and jumped onto the desk between us, hissing up a storm.

"What? Where did he come from?" Sandra demanded, turning redder and redder as each moment passed.

"Why don't you answer my question first," I

shouted at her. "I know you killed the Hayeses, and I can prove it!"

"You can't prove anything," she spat. "Now get out of here!"

I crossed my arms over my chest and stared straight into her eyes, hoping she couldn't see how afraid I was in that moment. "I'm not going anywhere until you admit what you did."

"I didn't do anything," she said, taking care to enunciate each word, but I was not convinced.

"You killed the Hayeses in cold blood. You bashed out their brains with a hammer and framed the handyman," I said. "Hey, if I agree to work with you, will you kill me, too?"

Sandra let out an enormous huff and lunged for me, but I was too fast for her.

I ran out of her office and back into the main waiting area. "Help!"

"No one else is here," Sandra told me, approaching slowly, deliberately.

I saw my chance, so I took it. Squeezing past her down the hall, I bolted back into her office and locked the door behind me.

"You're going to regret that!" she screamed, pounding furiously on the door.

I tuned her out and began pulling open drawers

and cabinets in search of evidence. "Help me find proof!" I told Octo-Cat, who sat licking his wounded tail.

Soon we were both tearing through the office.

Surely something had to be here.

"I called your mother just like you said," my tabby informed me.

"I'm calling the police!" Sandra screamed from the hallway.

"Good, that will make it easier for them to arrest you!" I shouted back, calling her bluff while shooting the cat an appreciative smile.

"Thanks for your help," I told him. "You did good."

We searched frantically for another couple moments, my desperation growing by the second.

"What's this? The words look familiar," Octo-Cat said, nudging a pile of mail from on top of the filing cabinet until it fell and scattered to the floor. He still didn't know how to read, but he was beginning to recognize familiar patterns of numbers and letters.

Sure enough, I combed through the pile and found a sealed envelope addressed to Charles at the firm.

"Oh! Think you can get away with blackmailing

my colleague, do you?" I called to Sandra, waving the letter around wildly even though she couldn't see it. "But why threaten him when you know perfectly well that Brock Calhoun didn't kill Bill and Ruth Hayes?"

She didn't come back at me with an angry retort. In fact, Sandra said nothing at all as the entire office fell silent. The only sound in my ears was my own blood as it flew through my veins at a rapid tempo. My heart went crazy as I sent up a silent prayer that Sandra hadn't somehow gotten her hands on a gun or some other weapon she could use to attack me through the closed door.

A moment later, the front door burst open, sending the greeting bell into a violent jangle.

"Laura Lee, Channel 7 News. Do you care to tell our viewers what's going on here?" my mother's voice rang out, loud and clear, and I could just picture her there with her probing microphone that she swung around like a sword when she was really on the warpath. I imagined now would be one of those times.

Feeling safe enough to exit now that I had backup, I swung the door open and stepped back into the main area just in time to see Sandra Lynn make a run for it.

"Mom! Stop her!" I screamed as I began to run after the fugitive. I had absolutely no idea what I would do if I caught her, but I at least had to try.

"Wait here," my mom said, dropping her mic and wrapping her arms around me. Her cameraman gave chase, but his gait was mired by the giant apparatus on his shoulder.

I watched through the glass door as a police car squealed to a stop and two armed officers jumped onto the scene.

"I've got her!" Charles called from somewhere I couldn't see.

My mom let go, and I raced outside to extend my view. Sure enough, Charles stood with the very distraught murderess in his embrace.

"You don't have any evidence!" she screamed.

"Actually, I have this," I said, waving the envelope in the air. "It was in her outgoing mail," I explained, handing it to the nearest officer.

"Threatening letters, huh?" the officer said with a smirk after scanning the letter. "Thanks for this," he told me as he slipped it into his pocket. "But the mass collusion and double homicide should be more than enough to put this one away for a long time."

"I have rights!" Sandra shouted pathetically.

"That's right," the other officer said. "Let me read them to you now. You have the right to remain silent..."

Charles ambled over to me with a bit of a limp, which made me think Sandra put up some kind of fight when he subdued her. "Are you okay?" he asked, checking me over.

"I'm fine."

Once he realized that was true, his handsome features contorted in an angry mask. "Why did you come out here on your own?"

"I had to find a way to prove Brock's innocence, and this seemed like the most surefire way."

"Well, it was the most ridiculous way," Charles said. "The most unsafe way, too."

I shook my head, going back over what the officer had said. "Did you find another way to prove she did it?"

He ran a hand through his hair and sighed. "Yes, and if you would have come back to the house, I could've told you that in person."

"How?" I insisted. I still couldn't figure out why the realtor had turned on her clients, and that was driving me crazy.

"Mitch," Charles said simply. "She set everything in motion by texting a few key people during our drive."

"But she said her phone—"

"She used Nan's," he cut me off. "Anyway, you were on the right track with the Bayside Printing Company, but you didn't have the right access. Bill's former employer, Mr. Weber, was able to do a system restore to recover previously deleted files. Once he knew to examine Lighthouse Realty & Brokerage's past jobs and records in particular, he found exactly what he was looking for."

I was so happy we'd found the answer, but it still didn't make sense to me. "Which was?"

"The motive," Charles said with a winning smile. "It was small and easy to miss, but on her latest print job, Sandra provided one page too many."

"Meaning?" I asked, motioning for him to hurry up and answer the question that had plagued me all week long.

"Meaning she gave Bill a financial document, which showed some illegal activity involving false documentation and offshore accounts," he explained.

"And so she killed him over that?" I asked. "Because she was worried he'd turn her in?"

"He blackmailed me!" Sandra screamed. "He said since I already knew how to skirt the rules that it shouldn't be a big deal to get him a new house free of charge, the selfish jerk! I didn't just have half a million to throw around. What was I supposed to do?"

"Not steal in the first place," one of the officers said as he pushed her head down and shoved her in the back of the cruiser.

"Yeah, and you definitely shouldn't have killed him or anybody else," the other said.

"Well, there you have it," my mom announced, coming to stand between me and Charles. "Brock Calhoun is innocent, and the real murderer has now been apprehended. And you saw it all unfold live, only on Channel 7."

As my mother began to interview Charles, I quietly slipped out of the frame and went to retrieve my cat and his iPad from inside the brokerage.

I found Octo-Cat curled up on Sandra's desk chair. Somehow he'd actually managed to fall asleep despite all that excitement.

"Hey." I nudged him awake gently. "We did it."

He blinked up at me, yawned, and then said, "Great. So what now?"

"How about a lobster roll from the Little Dog Diner?"

* * *

Charles joined us for lobster rolls and he even paid for everyone, including Mitch, Nan, and Yo-Yo who all joined us shortly after Sandra's arrest. I let him recount all the gritty details while I focused on the delicious meal before me.

Toward the end of his explanation, Nan hit me on the back of the head, almost causing me to choke again.

"What?" I cried, my mouth still stuffed with food.

"If you do something that stupid again, I'm going to kill you," she said, fixing me with a scowl.

"Sorry," I muttered. "Does Brock know yet?" I asked in an effort to change the subject to happier outcomes.

Charles licked a bit of mayo from his thumb. "They're processing him for release now. He'll be a free man by nightfall."

This news made me so happy I couldn't help but smile as I devoured a second lobster roll.

Mitch finished eating first, then picked Yo-Yo up and sat him on her lap. That reminded me of something that still didn't sit well with me.

"When I was talking with Sandra," I said, waiting for a beat to make sure everyone was listening, "she mentioned dog-sitting for a friend once. Do you think it's possible she meant Yo-Yo?"

"Do you really think she stole him, kept him hostage for a few weeks, and then let him go? That seems kind of improbable," Charles said. "What reason would she have for doing that?"

"Let's ask the dog," Octo-Cat said before taking a giant hunk of shrimp into his mouth.

"Would you?" I said, adding "please" when he didn't immediately comply.

"What's—?" Charles began, but I shushed him while I waited for the animals to finish their exchange.

"Affirmative," Octo-Cat said a moment later. "She took him that night when he wouldn't stop barking, but he got away and came home. It took him a while to find his way back from Misty Harbor, but he was determined to get home, no matter what."

I quickly relayed this information to the rest of the group.

"So, why didn't she kill him, too?" Charles asked, stating the obvious.

"I guess even evil has its limits," Nan said with a pert nod.

"He says he's sorry for not remembering everything sooner," Octo-Cat informed me. "And he said thank you for helping his family."

"What's going to happen to Yo-Yo now?" I asked the others.

"Charles is helping me petition the school to keep him with me on campus as an emotional support animal," Mitch answered with a sad smile. "I just couldn't imagine losing him again. He's the only family I have left now."

"And until then, he'll stay with me," Charles said. "But we should have no problem getting our petition approved, in light of..." His voice trailed off, but Mitch picked up the thread for him.

"My parents being recently murdered."

"What a day," Nan said with a giant sigh. "Let's take a break before investigating our next big case, if that's okay with you," she said, turning to me.

"What makes you think there will be a next case?" I asked, surprised.

"Because, my darling, you might not always go

about things in the safest way, but I think you've finally found your true calling."

"Which is?"

"You're the best private eye in all of Maine," she said with a proud smile.

"I'll drink to that," Charles said, raising his glass of soda.

"Me too," Mitch said.

That's when Mom came swooping into the restaurant to join us. "I'm here!" she cried. "What did I miss?"

"Nothing," Nan said, sending a wink my way. "Nothing at all."

Well, I guess I could tell Mom later. I'd had more than enough excitement that night already.

Octo-Cat nudged me with his paw. "Now that that's over with, I'm ready to collect on my favor."

Mom was busy giving her order to the waitress, so I bent down and quietly hissed, "What is it?"

"I want you to buy me a house," he said with a Cheshire grin.

"A house!" I exploded.

He nodded excitedly. "And not just any house. *My* house. I want to go home."

My jaw hung open as I searched for the appropriate response. Nothing came to me, though.

"Don't worry, you're coming, too," Octo-Cat added in a futile effort to answer my objections. He'd learned a lot about human society lately—I'd give him that—but there were certain things that still went way over his head, money being a prime example.

"You want me to just buy Ethel's house?" I hissed again. " There's no way I can afford that huge place."

"We'll figure out the details later," he assured me, returning his attention to his meal.

When I glanced back at my human dining companions, I saw Mom staring at me with a look I instantly recognized.

She knew.

These two cats are naked and afraid... But did they also kill their owner?

CLICK HERE to get your copy of *Hairless Harassment,* so that you can keep reading this series today!

* * *

And make sure you're on Molly's list so that you hear about all the new releases, monthly giveaways, and other cool stuff (including lots and lots of cat pics).

You can do that here:
MollyMysteries.com/subscribe

WHAT'S NEXT?

I never signed up to be a private investigator with a snarky, talking cat for a partner, but there's no backing down now. Especially considering a prominent politician was murdered pretty much right in my backyard.

The only witnesses were the senator's two hairless cats, Jacques and Jillianne. Normally pets want to help us solve their owner's murders, but this time it seems the two devious felines might actually be the ones who committed it...

Surprisingly enough, my own partner in crime, Octo-Cat, actually wants to help this time, but he can barely understand our two prime suspects because of their strange Sphynx accents. And I thought speaking tabby was hard!

So, there you have it, even with two successful cases behind me, I really don't know how I'm going to solve this one. Is it too late to go back and pick another career?

Hairless Harassment is now available.

CLICK HERE to get your copy so that you can keep reading this series today!

SNEAK PEEK OF HAIRLESS HARASSMENT

Hi, I'm Angie Russo, and my pet cat never ever stops talking. Not just mews and meows, but actual words that I can understand. So far, I'm the only one who seems to have this ability, and I still have absolutely no idea why.

It all started when I got zapped by a faulty coffee maker at the law firm where I work as a paralegal. Since then, Octo-Cat and I have used our special connection to solve two murder investigations together. Yeah, even I have to admit, we make a pretty great team.

Only a few weeks have passed since our super sleuthing earned the local handyman Brock Calhoun a *get-out-of-jail-free* card. And already my feline sidekick is begging for another case. Apparently, napping and complaining all day isn't an exciting enough life for him now.

All my life I've been on the search for that one amazing talent that would make me special and give me purpose. My nan starred on Broadway in her prime, and my parents both work for the local news station and love what they do.

They were all so sure of their talents early in life, but I've really struggled to pinpoint mine. I couldn't even figure out my passion well enough to nail down a bachelor's degree, racking up seven associate degrees instead.

I definitely never expected to find my true calling as a paralegal, especially considering how much I've always hated lawyers. But now that I have Octo-Cat and my special ability, I find that working at the offices of Thompson, Longfellow & Associates provides the perfect way to use my new-found abilities for good—especially considering that the newest partner knows all about my ability to speak to animals.

Oh, yeah! Charles didn't get fired. Instead, he got promoted. I was so proud of him that I even suggested we go back to the Little Dog Diner in Misty Harbor to celebrate with the world's best lobster rolls. He told me it would have to be some other time, though, because he already had plans with his new girlfriend, Breanne Calhoun.

Yeah, I don't get that, either.

The news that he'd started dating the cold and snippy realtor we'd very recently suspected of murder was enough to extinguish my crush on Charles once and for all, though. I've also decided that the next time Octo-Cat refers to him as "Upchuck," I'm not going to correct him.

The thought of him and Breanne together makes me sick, too.

It's for the best, though, I suppose. I really need to focus on understanding my new pet-whispering abilities, and Octo-Cat and I both need to get better at investigating cases without raising the community's suspicions. That pretty much means I have no time left for love or infatuation or whatever it was I once felt for Charles.

Anyway, who needs a boyfriend when you have a talking cat?

Not me. Well, at least not for right now.

Lately I've been spending a lot more time with my mom. Ever since she helped us catch the real murderer in our latest case, she's been on this kind of career high. She got the exclusive scoop and even managed to record our showdown with the murderer live and on camera. The feature was picked up all over the nation, and she and my dad have received job offers from clear across the country.

The latest was from San Antonio, I think.

She's not saying yes to any of them, though. At least, not unless I agree to move with them, too. But I would never leave Nan, and Nan would never leave Blueberry Bay.

So we're all staying put exactly where we are.

Sure, if enough people learn my secret, I probably will have to leave eventually. Right now, a total of five people know—Nan and my parents, who I told on purpose, along with Charles Longfellow, III and a college student named Mitch, who both figured it out by accident. Hopefully I can keep that number from growing any larger, but it seems like several people are on the verge of figuring things out already.

And that definitely worries me.

Especially since my mom just invited me to help her with her newest investigative journalism assignment...

* * *

I'd finally switched to a part-time schedule at the firm, and today was one of my days off. And by off, I meant I got to stay home and pack up my tiny rental house under the supervision of one very demanding tabby.

Not only did I have to discard a number of my belongings that he found to be inadequate, but he was also the reason I had to move in the first place. Granted, I'm the one who said I'd owe him a big favor if he allowed me to put him in a harness to take him outside. I hadn't counted on that favor amounting to more than six-thousand square feet, though.

As it turned out, the favor he wanted was for me to purchase the old manor house he had lived in with Ethel Fulton before she was murdered and, through a truly unbelievable series of events, he came to live with me. Now a twelve-dollar harness was costing me the better part of my five-thousand-dollar monthly stipend, and I'd learned to be more careful about promising my kitty companion open-ended favors.

Yes, my former boss, Richard Fulton, did offer me a generous break on the price. Also, there were fewer interested parties once the greater populace found that the former homeowner had been murdered, but still—*still!*—owning Fulton Manor would require a pretty penny from me not just to keep up with the mortgage, but also to carry out the many repairs that seemed to be more or less essential for safety purposes.

At least that's what the home inspector said.

Hardly any time has passed at all, and yet somehow the sale is final and the house is ready for me and Octo-Cat to move in. It's funny how bureaucracy can either slow things way down or speed them way up depending what side you approach the red tape from. Around Blueberry Bay, the Fultons owned the spool from which the red tape was unraveled, which meant I bought myself a manor house with very little effort on my part.

Nan, who adores both me and my cat in equal measure, decided to help out, too. Even though she'd owned her little Cape Cod style home for more than thirty-five years, she decided it was time to sell and move in with me at my new Eastern seaboard mansion.

"The difference is," she explained, "this time I'll be living with you and not the other way around." That was how she justified kicking me out of her house less than a year ago, only to move in with me now.

Honestly, I'm more than a little thrilled to have an added buffer when it comes to Octo-Cat. I love him more than anything, but he also infuriates me on a regular basis, constantly finding new and exciting ways to push the poorly constructed boundaries I've tried to erect.

And so all of us are moving in this weekend, even though Nan hasn't even had an offer on her house yet. Breanne says it will be easier to sell without a current resident. Yes, I couldn't believe Nan hired Calhoun Realty to list her house, either. She and I needed to have a serious talk about family loyalty.

But first we had to survive the big move.

"Someone just pulled up outside," Octo-Cat informed me, hopping onto the end of the bed where the better part of my wardrobe was laid out for evaluation. I took packing as a good opportunity to downsize, even though my living space would increase nearly ten times.

A moment later an urgent knock sounded on the front door and my mom's voice called out, "Angie? Angie, are you here?"

"Coming!" I yelled, letting the half-full box in my arms fall to the floor.

I flipped the deadbolt and my mom immediately

pushed her way inside. "You'll never guess what happened!" she told me, reaching into my closet and grabbing one of my jackets, which she thrust at me excitedly.

"What?" I asked, still a bit sleepy and not quite ready for this level of enthusiasm.

She followed me into the kitchen where I grabbed a can of Diet Mountain Dew and flipped the tab. It was my latest attempt at a suitable coffee replacement, and so far, so good.

"Lou Harlow was murdered!" she squealed with delight.

"Um, Mom. How about a little less bliss over someone dying, please?" Lou Harlow wasn't just some random local, either. As one of the two senators appointed to represent the great state of Maine, she was one of the most famous people to reside in our little corner of Blueberry Bay.

And now she was dead. And for some reason, my mother was terribly excited about it.

"I'm sorry. I know it's sad she died and everything, but guess who's been asked to cover it?" She bit her lower lip and pointed both thumbs toward her chest while widening her eyes to a comical degree.

"Congrats," I murmured, still feeling icky about her reaction to this whole thing.

"Thank you," she said with an airy smile. "Turns out I did such a great job covering the Hayes murders, the station would like me to do another investigative piece."

"I'm really happy for you, Mom." And I was. She'd worked hard to get here, and at last everything was coming up... bodies in the morgue, I guess.

"Good, because I need you to do it with me."

"What? No, no, no, no." Yeah, I'd done the legwork to find the Hayes's real killer and clear Brock Calhoun's name, but that didn't mean I wanted to jump straight into another murder investigation, especially one as prominent as this one would no doubt prove to be.

"Angie, I don't really think you have a choice."

I groaned and shook my head. "Oh, yeah, because that's the way to win me over."

"The senator was killed in her home," she revealed. "Do you know where that home is?"

"Somewhere in Glendale?" I guessed with a sigh.

"Not just somewhere," my mom corrected with

a new light dancing in her hazel eyes. "Right next door to your new house."

What happens next?
Don't wait to find out...

Purchase your copy so that you can keep reading this zany mystery series today!

MORE MOLLY

ABOUT MOLLY FITZ

While USA Today bestselling author Molly Fitz can't technically talk to animals, she and her doggie best friend, Sky Princess, have deep and very animated conversations as they navigate their days. Add to that, five more dogs, a snarky feline, comedian husband, and diva daughter, and you can pretty much imagine how life looks at the Casa de Fitz.

Molly lives in a house on a high hill in the Michigan woods and occasionally ventures out for good food, great coffee, or to meet new animal friends.

Writing her quirky, cozy animal mysteries is

pretty much a dream come true, but sometimes she also goes by the names Melissa Storm and Mila Riggs and writes a very different kind of story.

Learn more, grab the free app, or sign up for her newsletter at **www.MollyMysteries.com**!

PET WHISPERER P.I.

Angie Russo just partnered up with Blueberry Bay's first ever talking cat detective. Along with his ragtag gang of human and animal helpers, Octo-Cat is determined to save the day... so long as it doesn't interfere with his schedule. Start with book 1, *Kitty Confidential*.

PARANORMAL TEMP AGENCY

Tawny Bigford's simple life takes a turn for the magical when she stumbles upon her landlady's murder and is recruited by a talking black cat named Fluffikins to take over the deceased's role as the official Town Witch for Beech Grove, Georgia. Start with book 1, **Witch for Hire**.

MERLIN THE MAGICAL FLUFF

Gracie Springs is not a witch... but her cat is. Now she must help to keep his secret or risk spending the rest of her life in some magical prison. Too bad trouble seems to find them at every turn! Start with book 1, **Merlin the Magical Fluff.**

THE MEOWING MEDIUM

Mags McAllister lives a simple life making candles for tourists in historic Larkhaven, Georgia. But when a cat with mismatched eyes enters her life, she finds herself with the ability to see into the realm of spirits... Now the ghosts of people long dead have started coming to her for help solving their cold cases. Start with book 1, **Secrets of the Specter**.

THE PAINT-SLINGING SLEUTH

Following a freak electrical storm, Lisa Lewis's vibrant paintings of fairytale creatures have started coming to life. Unfortunately, only she can see and communicate with them. And when her mentor turns up dead, this aspiring artist must turn amateur sleuth to clear her name and save the day with only these "pigments" of her imagination to help her. Start with book 1, **My Colorful Conundrum**.

SPECIAL COLLECTIONS

Black Cat Crossing
Pet Whisperer P.I. Books 1-3
Pet Whisperer P.I. Books 4-6
Pet Whisperer P.I. Books 7-9
Pet Whisperer P.I. Books 10-12

CONNECT WITH MOLLY

Sign up for my newsletter and get a special digital prize pack for joining, including an exclusive story, Meowy Christmas Mayhem, fun quiz, and lots of cat pictures!

mollymysteries.com/subscribe

Have you ever wanted to talk to animals? You can chat with Octo-Cat and help him solve an exclusive online mystery here:

mollymysteries.com/chat

Or maybe you'd like to chat with other animal-loving readers as well as to learn about new books and giveaways as soon as they happen! Come join Molly's VIP reader group on Facebook.

mollymysteries.com/group

MORE BOOKS LIKE THIS

Welcome to Whiskered Mysteries, where each and every one of our charming cozies comes with a furry sidekick... or several! Around here, you'll find we're all about crafting the ultimate reading experience. Whether that means laugh-out-loud antics, jaw-dropping magical exploits, or whimsical journeys through small seaside towns, you decide.

So go on and settle into your favorite comfy chair and grab one of our *paw*some cozy mysteries to kick off your next great reading adventure!

Visit our website to browse our books and meet our authors, to jump into our discussion group, or to join our newsletter. See you there!

www.WhiskeredMysteries.com

Printed in Great Britain
by Amazon

17391177R00153